BLOOD FAMILY

www.totallyrandombooks.co.uk

Also by Anne Fine

Published by Corgi Books:

The Book Of The Banshee • *The Granny Project*
On The Summerhouse Steps • *The Road Of Bones* • *Round Behind The Ice House*
The Devil Walks • *The Stone Menagerie* • *Up On Cloud Nine*

Published by Corgi Yearling Books:

Bad Dreams • *Charm School* • *Frozen Billy*
The More The Merrier • *Eating Things On Sticks* • *Trouble in Toadpool*

A Shame to Miss . . .
Three Collections Of Poetry
Perfect Poems For Young Readers • *Ideal Poems For Middle Readers*
Irresistible Poetry For Young Adults

Other books by Anne Fine

For junior readers:

The Angel Of Nitshill Road • *Anneli The Art-Hater*
Bill's New Frock • *The Chicken Gave It To Me* • *The Country Pancake*
Crummy Mummy And Me • *Genie, Genie, Genie*
How To Write Really Badly • *Ivan The Terrible*
The Killer Cat's Birthday Bash • *The Killer Cat Runs Away*
Loudmouth Louis • *A Pack Of Liars* • *Stories Of Jamie And Angus*

For young people:

Flour Babies • *Goggle-Eyes* • *Madame Doubtfire*
Step By Wicked Step • *The Tulip Touch* • *Very Different*

For adult readers:

All Bones And Lies • *Fly In The Ointment* • *The Killjoy*
Raking The Ashes • *Taking The Devil's Advice*
Telling Liddy • *Our Precious Lulu* • *In Cold Domain*

www.**annefine**.co.uk

BLOOD FAMILY

ANNE FINE

DOUBLEDAY

BLOOD FAMILY

A DOUBLEDAY BOOK 978 0 857 53240 4

First published in Great Britain by Doubleday,
an imprint of Random House Children's Publishers UK
A Random House Group Company

This edition published 2013

1 3 5 7 9 10 8 6 4 2

The Random House Group Limited supports the Forest Stewardship Council®
(FSC®), the leading international forest-certification organisation. Our books carrying
the FSC label are printed on FSC®-certified paper. FSC is the only forest-certification
scheme supported by the leading environmental organisations, including Greenpeace.
Our paper procurement policy can be found at www.randomhouse.co.uk/environment.

MIX
Paper from
responsible sources
FSC® C016897

Set in Bembo

Doubleday Books are published by Random House Children's Publishers UK,
61-63 Uxbridge Road, London, W5 5SA

www.**randomhousechildrens**.co.uk
www.**totallyrandombooks**.co.uk
www.**randomhouse**.co.uk

Addresses for companies within The Random House Group Limited can be found at:
www.**randomhouse**.co.uk/offices.htm

THE RANDOM HOUSE GROUP Limited Reg. No. 954009

A CIP catalogue record for this book is available from the British Library.

Printed and bound in Great Britain by Clays Ltd, St Ives plc

In memoriam
Fred McFeely Rogers

Eddie

None of them would believe me if I told them. So I say nothing. I don't lie, but I don't come out with it. Most of the people who teach me assume I come from the same sort of home as all the others. They don't know who I am and, if they did, most of them would have forgotten the headlines. It was all years ago.

It started with a banging on the door. 'Open up. Police! Open this door, please.'

Mum made a mousy noise from fright, and curled herself deeper in the chair, digging out more of the stuffing with her nails. On went the banging. On and on. But there was something odd about the way the voice outside stayed calm. 'Open up, please!' It didn't get louder or angrier. In fact, it sounded almost tired, as if whoever was calling to us through the door had never been expecting any response.

'We know you're in there, Mrs Harris. Please open up. Nobody's going to harm you.'

I do remember thinking *that* was mad. What did they

reckon was going to happen to her after Harris came home, if she unlocked the door? He had his rules, and not letting anyone in was pretty well the most important – apart from keeping quiet all the time, and never fidgeting or asking questions.

The voice changed tack. 'Edward?' There was a pause. Perhaps it struck him I might not be called that, because he tried again. 'Eddie? Ed? Are you in there with your mother?'

I looked her way. But she'd shrunk even deeper in the chair and buried her face in her arms.

'Right, then.' The voice was still patient. 'Mrs Harris? Eddie? Stand well away from the door because we're going to have to force it open from this side.'

I didn't see how it was possible. Every time Harris left the flat, Mum had to slide both bolts across, and slip on both the chains. But almost at once I heard the rasp of metal. Someone was jemmying the door on the hinge side. I knew then they'd be in within a minute. After all, Harris had said it often enough when he was cursing the rattling window frames or cupboard doors that wouldn't shut. 'Whoever jerry-built these flats ought to be boiled in oil!'

There was the most almighty splintering noise.

And they were in.

Five of them. That surprised me, for we'd heard only one voice. I suppose the others had kept quiet so that we didn't think they were some mob from one of the clubs, coming for money Harris owed. Three were police – two burly men and one tall woman. But there were two more behind: one soft-looking, halfway-to-bald man, and one young woman with bright copper hair.

All of them stared at me. 'Well, well!' one muttered. 'So the old lady was right.'

I felt peculiar. I wasn't used to meeting people's eyes because Mum hardly ever raised hers from the floor, and I would always try to keep my face turned well away from Harris in case it set him off.

They looked around the room. The younger woman with the blazing hair tugged out a fistful of tissues and pressed them to her nose. 'What is that *smell*?' But no one answered her because the officer who had been telling us to open the door was already asking, 'When is Bryce Harris expected back?'

The question was directed at me. Not one of them had done much more than glance at my mother, and she had buried herself so deeply in the chair you couldn't even see what Harris had left of her hair.

I shook my head. I didn't know when he was coming home. Sometimes we got ourselves into a state for nothing, fearing that someone else's grinding footsteps up the stairs belonged to him. But often he was back quite soon, as if to catch us out.

The man who wasn't in a uniform dropped to his knees in front of where I was crouching. 'That must have been a bit of a fright,' he said. 'I'm sorry if you got scared.'

I didn't say a word.

'My name is Rob,' he said. 'Rob Reed, and I'm a social worker.' He waved towards the woman. 'So is this lady here. And I need to explain that you can't stay here any more. So, for the moment, we'll be taking you out of this flat with us.'

I'm sure I stared. I hadn't been out of the flat since Harris made us move here because some woman from my nursery school kept coming round to talk to Mum.

He peered at me more closely. 'Eddie? Edward? Do you understand what I'm saying?'

I must have nodded since, with some relief, he pushed his hands down on his knees to lever himself upright. 'You're not to worry,' he assured me. 'Your mother will be coming along.' Unsure, he turned to the others. 'Right?'

I realized everyone was looking at the bruises down Mum's legs. One of the officers muttered, 'Too right. Can't leave her here to get another royal kicking.' He nodded to the women. 'Best get her out of here.'

They stepped a little further into the room and leaned over my mother, who whimpered as they prised her fingers from her face and held her under the arms. One of the other officers turned to me. 'Can you stand up, lad?'

I pushed my back against the wall and up, till I was on my feet. I saw him staring at the greasy black smudge behind me on the wallpaper, and realized for the very first time how many hundreds of times I must have cowered against that wall till, desperate not to call attention to myself, I dared slide up it in that quiet way.

'Got anything to wear?'

I looked down at myself. I don't suppose I'd thought about the clothes I wore, until that moment. But I watch television so I knew what he was thinking of the state of me.

'Here,' said the man who'd called himself Rob Reed, noticing my confusion. 'I'll look for something.'

'Don't hang about,' the elder officer warned. 'I'm sure we'd all prefer to get away before trouble arrives.'

I think we all knew what he meant by 'trouble'. Already Mum was halfway to the door, stumbling between the women. Her head was down. She didn't look to see if I was following. The younger officer left as well, but only to see the three of them safely down the stairs because he was soon back. The radio clipped to his jacket was chirruping as he came through the door, and I distinctly heard the words 'safe in the van'.

Rob Reed opened the door to the small room that used to be my bedroom till Harris said he needed it to store some stuff. I suppose he thought I must have clothes in there. He saw the great black plastic bag and turned to me. 'So what's in there?'

I didn't see that there was any point in lying. 'Harris's dog.'

'His *dog*?'

I wasn't sure how to explain. 'He said that he would get her out of here when he had time.'

'It stinks! It absolutely stinks!' he said, though I thought Gem had been bagged up so long it wasn't too bad. And I was used to the smell.

He yanked the cupboard door open – 'Oh, my Lord!' – and slammed it shut again before more bottles could come tumbling out. Then he turned back to me. 'Don't you have *any* other clothes?'

I shook my head. I mean, I had pyjamas, but even I knew they were probably worse.

As if his sheer disgust had made him brave, Rob Reed strode into the room where Harris sleeps. (Mum uses the big chair.) He yanked a shirt off a hook. 'Put this on.'

Then he saw my face.

'Listen,' he said, 'you're safe now. He can't get at you any more.'

We went back in the telly room. He pointed to the blanket in the corner. 'Is this where you've been *sleeping*?'

I nodded. And suddenly you could tell that all he wanted was to get out of there. I think he recognized his own rising anger as quickly as I had. Looking around the room, he asked me almost roughly, 'Is there *anything* in here you want to keep?' But I was back against the wall again, down on my heels, and had no answer.

I watched the two of them through the gap I kept cut in my fringe so I could see when Harris had calmed down enough for me to move. Their eyes met and the officer nodded towards the door. Rob Reed looked desperately round the room. But it was all spilled ashtrays, empty bottles, and one or two chipped ornaments from when Mum and I lived in the other place – the one with flowers and that stringy rug I liked to pick at. I saw his eyes run over the newspaper Harris had taped across the window – 'to stop that nosy old bat across the way prying into our lives' – and past the broken lamp and torn town map. Beside the telly was a mess of tangled wires, and all of Harris's nasty games and films and stuff were out of their boxes, all over.

Rob Reed looked at the table. Empty packets of cigarettes, a few more bottles and a heap of newspapers.

He reached down. Propping up one leg was an old book – a musty thing covered in dark green leather. Harris had swiped it from a market stall after he had upended the table in a temper one night, snapping the end off one of its legs. The book meant nothing to me. I knew my letters – anybody would who'd watched as much telly as I had. But I couldn't read; and anyway, once Harris jammed it underneath the table leg, nobody in their right mind would have dared touch it.

Rob Reed said, 'Maybe this is yours?' and from the hopeful – almost desperate – way he asked the question I guessed that finding something that was mine was part of his job, and we would not be able to leave until he had.

Right then, I heard men shouting. It sounded muffled and far away, so could have been from any of the blocks.

But I still panicked as I always do, and held my hand out for the book as if I wanted it, so we could all get out of there before Harris came back.

He read the title on the spine out loud before he passed it over. '*The Devil Ruled the Roost.*'

The police officer cast one last look around the flat and shivered. Their eyes met once again. Then I heard Rob Reed muttering quietly to himself as he steered me in front of him towards the door. 'Didn't he just? Oh, yes indeed. Didn't he just!'

Betty – Flat 420D

I noticed the police car parked across the road the moment I looked out of my window. It was unmarked, but I knew all of them. It was no later than half past six. I can't think why they thought Bryce Harris might be up that early. If anyone's a night bird, it's him. The club he hangs about in doesn't shut till God knows when, so he is rarely out and about much before noon.

That's when I used to see the child – before Bryce Harris got up. I'd watch the waif's face flattened hopefully against the window, longing for something to see, aching for something interesting to happen. That was before that overgrown criminal bastard caught sight of me across the yard one day, and stuck that newspaper all over. For just a week or two I'd sometimes see the corner of the paper twitch, as if the boy was still shoving his face close enough to try to see out, maybe with only one eye. But then one day that side was taped down even more thoroughly. You saw the shadow of the mess Harris had clearly made, doing the job in a temper. And since there were no windows on the other side, I don't suppose that, after that, the child saw anything except his own thin life.

That's why I wrote the letter. It was quite obvious he'd get no help from his mother. She was a drab and hopeless thing who'd had the stuffing punched out of her all right. Everyone said so. When she and Harris first moved in to 314B, she used to creep out sometimes to nip down to Ali's on the corner. I saw her in the queue there more than once and always took the chance to peep in her basket. Sausage rolls close to their date stamp. The cheapest cheese and bread. Pies. Cigarettes and cans of beer. It wasn't much on which to feed a growing child. Small wonder that the small mite's face always looked pasty.

I wondered why she never took the boy along with her. He could at least have carried back the toilet rolls, and he'd have had a breath of air. But then I heard a whisper that the three of them had done a flit from their last place, and so I guessed they kept the boy well hidden because, once people see a child who isn't in a nursery or school, tongues start to wag.

I took a lot of care with my first letter. I know how stupid people can be, letting out names, and no one would have wanted Bryce Harris to find out that they'd

11

interfered in any aspect of his life. And so, although I write as neatly as anyone my age who can still hold a pen, and spell not just better than most, but well enough to have won prizes all through school, I found a grubby sheet of paper and wrote the scruffiest letter, almost along the lines of all those ransom notes you see in films where every letter has been cut out separately from magazines and newspapers, then stuck in wobbly lines across the page.

Theirs a boy in 314B, I wrote. *They keep him hiden away, but he needs HELP.*

I waited for Thursday, when the woman from the Social comes in to visit Mrs McGuire. She stays for twenty minutes every time. Never a moment more or less. So with a minute or two to spare, I stuck it on the lift with tape, and scuttled back in my flat. I kept my ears pinned back. Nobody else came up or down. So when the woman had gone and I popped out to check, the note had vanished and I knew for sure she must have taken it.

And nothing happened. I tried to be patient, but by then the child was worrying me all day and half the night, and so I tried again. This time I wrote a proper letter, put it in a proper envelope and gave a nice-looking boy outside the Social offices a pound to give it to the man at the reception desk. I even stood there lurking under my umbrella until I'd seen the envelope change hands.

Still, there was no response.

In my third letter I was a good deal tougher. I said that everyone in the flats was worried sick about this child and knew he'd been reported to them more than once. I said two separate journalists had told us that responsibility for his death would be laid at the Social Services' door if they didn't send someone round to check on him at once. (I had no reason to think the boy was starving or anything, but I did think the threat of it might stir them into action.)

It still took them eleven days to get their skates on. I had been planning to send a different note, to the police this time, to say that guns were kept at No. 314B. Everyone knows that talking about guns wakes that lot up. We have a story round here that some woman in B flats phoned the police about a burglary taking place across the way only to hear the lad on the desk replying that he was sorry but no officers were free to deal with her complaint.

'It isn't a complaint,' she said. 'It is a *burglary*, going on right this minute. These boys are kicking the door in.'

'Sorry,' the lad said. 'Saturday's a busy night. We don't have anyone free.'

So she just added, 'I think they've got guns.'

In less than half a minute she was hearing sirens. Squad cars surrounded the place. Megaphones. Uproar. Everyone herded out. She got a serious ticking off. They even threatened to put her on a charge. 'Why did you *lie*?'

the officer demanded. 'Why did you tell us they were *armed*?'

'Who was it started with the lies?' she snapped back. 'It was you who said that you had no one free. Now look at the bloody swarm of you! Don't you dare start on me!'

But I'd heard all about how many guns were waved about that night. I didn't want there to be any accidents. So I held off and, sure enough, finally someone from Social Services took notice of my threatening letter and managed to stir stumps enough to come and look.

And they had clearly done a bit of homework first. A series of unmarked cars sat there all morning, then through my lunch-time snack. They knew enough to wait till Harris had gone. I saw him leave while I was steeping tea, sometime around two. He shambled over the yard as usual, the giant oaf, and less than ten minutes later another squad car cruised to a halt in front of B flats. I saw the five of them go through the door.

And then I waited. It was seventeen minutes by the clock before two of them led the mother out. My Christ, she was a mess. The woman could barely keep her feet shuffling between them, although they held her up. Her scalp was bald in patches, perhaps from the stress of living with that bully. More likely he had torn it out in one of his famous flare-ups. The car ticked over for a minute or two, and then, as if it had been waiting for yet another squad car that drew up behind, it did a turnabout, and left.

From then on I was sure — sure as I'm writing this — that what I'd see next would be one of the other officers carrying out that poor boy's body, wrapped in a filthy blanket. I never touched the tea. I just stared, worried that if I even blinked I might miss what was happening.

Then this plump, balding, fatherly man led out the boy. The child came through the double doors and startled like a horse. It wasn't even all that sunny, but he blinked hard in the light. I don't believe he could have been much more than seven years old. He looked about the sort of height my Harry was when he moved from the infants to the junior school.

Someone inside the squad car swung the door open as the two of them came close. I knew the bloke who'd fetched the boy out of the flats could not be a policeman because he didn't shove the boy's head down as he pushed him in the car, the way they do. (You learn a lot about police habits when you live round here.) The boy clambered in the back as clumsily as if he wasn't even sure which way he would be facing when he got inside.

The car door shut as one last officer rushed out of the flats to join the driver in the front. And then they drove away.

'Job well done, Betty!' I congratulated myself and, looking down, reckoned that I deserved a brand-new mug of tea. One hot and fresh, not stewed and stone-cold like the one sitting in front of me.

15

I put the kettle on again then, trembling, sat at the kitchen table and wept my heart out with relief.

PC Martin Tallentire

I won't try saying that I'd never seen the like before, because I had. By then I'd been in the police force for eleven years. I'd been the first to reach road accidents. I'd seen boys who'd been daft enough to tangle with rough-house drunks, and I'd rolled tramps and homeless druggies over in doorways, only to find them frozen stiff. I'd held down the flap on a girl's bleeding face after a trivial cat fight turned into a full-on duel with broken bottles, and was at Mr Templeton's the day the housing officers finally managed to winkle him out. (That was an object lesson in how much filth and garbage one mad man can fit in a one-bedroom flat.)

But I had never seen a sight quite like that woman. She was barely human any more. That bastard had ripped out so much of her hair that she was halfway to scalped. I thought at first the thin, weird keening I could hear was coming from that armchair – as if someone had left one of those joke rubber bags leaking under the cushion.

Then I saw her leg move. I didn't recognize it as a leg at first, because of the way it twitched. And it was black. Christ knows, I've seen some bruises in my time. Nursed some myself, after the odd weekend round-up of revellers at the far end of Marley Road. But livid flesh like that – green, blue, purple, yellow, black. The woman was a rainbow in herself. That Harris must have gone at her pretty well every night. Small wonder she was just a cowering bag of torn clothes in a chair.

Strange job, this. We deal with all types, all ages. Posh ones who ask you in and patronize you as they make you tea. Loudmouths who jeer as you pass. Toe-rags who hurl rocks at the car from around corners. You have to learn to keep the world from getting under your skin. But every now and again you'll see a small kid breaking his heart in a doorway, or some poor sod who just walked down the wrong street at the wrong time and had his head kicked in. And you'll just want to pack in the whole boiling, go home and weep.

That's how I felt that day. Partly the stink of the place! Hard to believe those two had lived in that flat, hour by hour, day by day, with that reek up their noses each breath they took. I nearly gagged. I watched that social worker – Rob, was it? – prowl round the poky place, looking for something better than that manky T-shirt and those raggy bottoms to cover the kid from prying eyes. And all I could think was, 'Get a move on, mate! I just want out of here. You can come back some other time to trawl around for your report.'

But, no. We had to wait while he peered into every cupboard. What he was looking for I couldn't think.

And then he pounces. On a *book*.

A book! I ask you. In that benighted, stinking hole.

I wonder about these social workers sometimes, truly I do.

Eddie

Outside hit me in the face, the slap of it against my skin. I had forgotten. And it smelled – oh, I don't know. Hard, somehow. Almost harsh. Like *crystal*. I think air shocked me almost more than light, and once or twice since, smelling chlorine as I've walked past swimming pools, I've been swept back to that strange moment when Rob opened the downstairs door.

I shan't forget the police-car ride: how big and wide the world looked. The road ran through the park, and all I could think of was my old nursery because there'd been a patch of green there. It was like seeing something half-forgotten. Of course there are trees and grass on television all the time. But seeing half a park of it on either side of you is something very different. My head was swimming with green.

And sky. Even before Harris covered up the windows, we were far enough down the flats that I had to twist my head to see even a slice of sky. The window in the car was closed, but if I leaned against it and looked up, I could see masses of blue.

Everything rushed past so quickly. And everywhere was so *bright*.

Because it was a police car, I thought that we were going to the station. (Mr Perkins once went to the station.) When the car stopped, Rob Reed said, 'We're here.' And when I didn't move, he leaned across to push the car door open. After I got out, he let me stand and stare a little while before he said, 'Come on, Eddie. Time enough for that later.'

This time I wasn't so slow because I knew for certain that he meant me. (I know that probably sounds as if I was thick as a brick. But Harris had only ever called me 'Stain' or 'Toe-rag', and Mum used to call me 'Sweetie' when she still spoke at all, so I had half forgotten that my name was Edward.)

Rob Reed led me to a glass door that startled me when it began to open before he even touched it. Behind it were more people than I had ever seen in my whole life. And not a single one of them was looking at me.

'Come on, Eddie,' Rob Reed said. 'We go this way.'

And then he led me down a corridor so long I thought we'd never reach the end.

Dr Ruth Matchett, Queen Anne Hospital

It was astonishing, really, how well he seemed. When I was told, before I went into the cubicle, that the boy had not been out of his flat for years I do remember thinking, 'Here we go. Vitamin deficiencies. Possible stunted growth. And no doubt so mentally impoverished he'll be halfway to retarded.'

There were a few faint bruises on his lower legs, as if the brute who kept on kicking him couldn't be arsed to raise his foot far from the floor, or put much effort into it. (I heard a different story about his mum. She'd been kicked halfway to pulp and was apparently so addled she could no longer speak.) The child had got off lightly. He did have one or two scars. But nothing you could pin down to a cigarette burn, or anything like that. I've seen far worse. Indeed, kids come in here looking a heap more battered than that after a rugby match.

He didn't speak. But he would answer questions, so it was clear his brain still worked. Mostly he shook his head, or nodded. But when an answer was necessary, as when I asked him, 'Can you tell me your name?' he shot a look at his minder – that nice, tubby, half-bald chap called Rob – and then came out with it all right. 'Eddie.'

I ran my eyes over his clothing. The shirt was huge and close to clean. But I couldn't even tell what he was wearing over his arse because it was such a rag. So I just said, 'Well, Eddie, I'm afraid we have to take this shirt away from you now.'

Rob muttered, 'He won't be sorry about that,' so drily that I guessed the shirt must have belonged to this Bryce Harris bloke that they'd arrested.

I eased off Eddie's clothes. That's when I thought I'd see real damage. These household bullies aren't daft. They often concentrate on places no one sees. But there were no marks on his trunk or buttocks. Rob Reed stretched out a hand to stroke his head while I did all the private checks that children hate – especially the kids who think they know what's coming after. Eddie did shrink from my touch. But I would guess that could be simple modesty. And I must say that I saw nothing on his body anywhere to lead me to assume he'd been abused that way.

He didn't even have nits.

We did take photographs, although I couldn't see them helping in any court case.

'No paperwork, I suppose?' I asked when we'd gone through the tests. 'No medical card or name of a family doctor, or anything?'

'Fat chance,' said Rob. 'They will send someone in tomorrow to take a better look. But I'm not hopeful. The place was a tip.'

'If you find nothing, then we'll have to start his shots again.' I made a note. 'He may have had his first few

21

before his mum took up with Sunshine.' I spoke directly to the child. 'Eddie, do you remember a doctor or a nurse ever giving you any injections? Sticking a needle in your arm and telling you that it would only hurt a tiny bit and it would soon be over?'

Either he didn't understand or didn't answer. He was staring at the polished floor. So I said, 'Never mind,' and peeled off my protective gloves. 'I think that's it for now.'

I wrapped the boy in one of our little furry dressing gowns so he could be taken along to the unit for something to eat and a bath while one of the hospital volunteers looked him out some fresh clothes. But at the door Rob stopped and looked back enquiringly. I shrugged. We do try not to talk about these children over their heads as though they were dead or unconscious. But Rob's a good man and he takes his job to heart, so I did want him to know that, so far as I could tell, there wasn't anything he couldn't see for himself. A few old bruises. That was it. I only wish that all the kids that poor man's brought in here had been so lucky.

Mind you, it's not my job to check the damage to the poor child's mind and sense of self.

That often never heals at all.

Eddie

When we came out again, the sun was so bright that it hurt my eyes, and I kept blinking. Rob Reed noticed that. (He noticed everything.) 'If that keeps up,' he said, 'we're going to have to take you to have your eyes checked right away.'

That seemed to make him think of something else. 'Ten-minute break in the park?' He grinned. 'Might as well seize the chance to start on the sunbathing.'

He stopped the car. 'Don't move,' he said, surprising me because I hadn't thought of it. 'I'm coming round to let you out the other side.' I could see why. The cars went whizzing by so fast they made me dizzy.

He took my hand and led me over lumpy grass. 'Sit facing this way.' He put me with my back to the sun. And when I felt my head and neck get hotter, I thought it was because the nurse who'd put me in the bath and cut my finger- and toenails must have done something odd to my hair when she was washing it. The things I didn't know back then, or put together wrong!

But I knew one thing. 'Shouldn't I have sun cream on?'

Rob raised an eyebrow – just a tiny bit; but if there's one thing I had learned, it was to read a face. I put my head down and picked at the grass.

It was a bit of time before he said, 'You think you should?'

It just popped out. 'Well, Mr Perkins said you *always* should.'

'Who's Mr Perkins?'

I recognized the over-casual voice. Seeing my mum with Harris had taught me well enough how one tiny thing let drop could be drawn out, and then blown up and up till even she believed she'd earned the kicking. So I said nothing, hoping he would let it go. But he persisted. 'Who's Mr Perkins, Eddie?'

Well *now*, of course, I know full well what he was probably thinking. So it is almost a laugh to think I felt so nervous about answering, 'You know. On telly.'

'On telly?'

'Yes. His show.'

'I've never seen it.'

And of course he hadn't. Those tapes were thirty years old. I don't know who had left them in that cupboard, but there they were, in piles of unmarked boxes. Mum and I put on the first tape one day when I was very young. Harris was still bad-tempered from the move, and he'd slammed out. Mum made me cocoa because I was upset from all his shouting. 'Maybe it's a film,' she said.

But it was Mr Perkins. Episodes of some old telly show. He came in, singing a song about feeling good because it was a new day, and there were all these things that we could do together.

'Happy days, and happy ways
I hope you know how glad I am
To see you here with me today
We're going to have great fun.'

While he was singing, he was taking off his jacket. It always started like that. Then he'd switch on the kettle and tip food into the cat's dish. ('Here you are, Sooty-Sue! My, weren't you hungry!') He'd show us what he'd been making out of toilet-roll holders and glue, or paper and string and some old plastic flowerpot, or something. Mr Perkins could use *anything*. And after that, we all went on a visit. Each show was different, but it was always interesting things. Mr Perkins would take us along to the fire station, or a farm, or a pizza parlour. ('Off we go. Jump on the bus with me.') We met a lady who shoed horses, and someone who drew cartoons. We saw how oranges were picked by huge machines with arms, and visited hospitals, and learned how they made spaghetti in a factory. Sometimes I worried that we would run out of people and places to visit, but we never did. And everywhere Mr Perkins took us, he asked a hundred questions. 'Why do you do it *that* way?' 'Do you ever get scared?' 'Is it difficult?' 'Have you ever burned yourself by mistake?' 'How long does it take to cook?'

He never ran out of questions. Sometimes he'd turn to us. 'Do *you* ever help with the cooking?' 'Have *you* ever had bad sunburn?' (That's how I knew about the cream.)

25

I'd always answer, even if I had my mouth stuffed full of pie or cheese. But in the end we'd say goodbye to whoever it was we had been visiting that day, and wave, and he would take us back to his house. Then he would sing another song about how we could grow up to do anything we wanted – anything at all. All it would take was for us to want to do that thing enough.

'Because you're strong and brave inside
But most of all, of course, because you want to,
Want to, want to
Because you're strong and brave inside
And really, really want to.'

When we had finished watching that first time, Mum rubbed the tear stains off her cheek and pressed a button so the tape slid out. She put it back in the box. 'Tell you what, why don't we put it safely back in the cupboard, out of sight, so we can watch it again some other day?'

I think, even back then, I must have known she meant, 'away from Bryce'. (She called him Bryce. And it was only after the hammerings on the door began practically every night – 'Where's Harris?' 'Harris, you bastard! Open up! You owe me money!' 'I know you're in there, Harris!' – that Mum got frightened and weird in her head, and then stopped talking, and I almost forgot his name used to be Bryce.)

I put the tape in the box. I was so proud to work out

that it had to go in facing the right way before the plastic case would shut. Mum put the box back on the pile in the cupboard and dropped one of her blouses on top. I suppose she thought, if Harris saw the tapes, he would record his own stuff over them. And even after Harris brought home his brand-new telly with the DVD, I kept them carefully in there and only played them on the old machine when he was out. I don't think Harris even realized that the box he dumped his six-packs on so they would be in reach still actually worked. If you're the sort of person who hasn't moved the body of your own dog out of the flat in weeks, why would you notice some out-of-date machine still gathering dust in the corner?

Robert Reed, Social Services

It was the first time we'd sat down to chat, there in the park that day. He looked all washed and clean. That nurse had done a brilliant job with Eddie's hair, disguising the bit he'd hacked away at the front by making the whole cut shorter. Not elfin. It was too much of a mop for that. But cute. (If I had a bit more hair, I'd go to her instead of to Luigi.) They'd put Eddie in a pair of grey trousers and a plain white shirt. I swear that, sitting there in dappled sunlight, we must have looked just like a normal little boy and his grandpa, chatting about nothing.

Except that Eddie kept craning round to look at

everything. A bird pecking the scruffy grass; something that rustled in the leaves above us; a toddler on a bike, over towards the swings. The raucous melody that came from the ice-cream van confused him till I told him what it was. (I doubt if any ice-cream vendor in this town is daft enough to take a van near to those flats.) Even the daisies amazed him.

He just sat quietly and stared. He was a serious little boy, and very wary. Like all too many of the kids I see, he startled far too easily. I'd tried the old tests that we're not supposed to use these days – slammed the car door behind him, raised my hand suddenly – that sort of thing. And, sure enough, each time the boy went rigid.

Still, there was something inside him that didn't seem to have been crushed. Of course, we didn't know how long his mum had been in that pathetic state. (With luck, not too much of the last four years.) But it was obvious we could do *something* with him.

That's why I chose the Radletts for that first night. They are the best on our No Notice list. I left young Eddie picking at the grass just like a curious toddler and, pulling out my phone, strolled out of hearing. 'Linda? Can I bring you another small gift tonight?'

'Oh, God!' she said. 'We've only just got shot of Gary.'

'I know. But this one's special.'

'Oh, aren't they all?'

We shared a cynical laugh. And then I said, 'So that's OK, then, is it?'

'I really ought to speak to Alan. He's still quite frayed. And he's not finished fixing the gate after young Gary's fond farewell.'

'This boy is nothing like Gary.'

'He'd better not be.' There was a pause. 'So can you tell me anything?'

'Later. By then I'll know a little more.'

She sighed. 'When should we expect him?'

I looked at my watch. Though I was starving it was only five. 'I'll take him back to the office now to try to get a few things straight. Then we'll come round. Say around six or seven?'

'We'll be here.'

Eddie

Rob kept his eye on me all through his phone call. Then he came back. 'Ready to go?'

We got in the car again. I can remember being really surprised because the ride went bumpy. At first I thought it was just holes in the road but then I heard him muttering, 'Bloody speed humps!'

The car drew up outside another building with glass doors, just like the hospital. Rob nodded at the man behind the desk, then steered me through some swing doors and along a corridor. Most of the people who passed us coming the other way nodded, but nobody stopped to talk. He tried a couple of doors, poking his head inside as soon as he'd knocked, only to end up muttering, 'Sorry,' and closing the door again.

Finally he came across an empty room and we went in. It had a brick-red carpet and armchairs, and there were toys on a low table and more in a heap in the corner. There was a mirror all along the wall and as Rob propelled me past it, to a chair, I thought a boy was walking in beside us. I didn't recognize the sideways glimpse of me.

Rob picked up the phone on the table and punched a number. I didn't understand what he said to the person at the other end, but someone else came in soon after that and sat down in the chair between us.

'Eddie,' he told me, 'this is Sue. She's a police officer, but she's a really good friend, and she is going to listen to what we talk about. She might have one or two questions of her own that she might want me to ask. And she's going to record what we are saying on this little machine.'

I hadn't noticed the machine. It was so small I'd taken it for some fancy silver cigarette packet left on the table.

'Just so we can remember things. Is that all right?' said Sue.

I didn't know if that was all right, did I? I didn't look at her. I just sat tight.

Then suddenly it was questions, questions, questions. What I thought strangest was how much they knew, but still kept asking about. They certainly seemed to know a lot about Harris, and they knew things I didn't know about my mum. Rob told me someone said she'd once worked in a dress shop and asked me if she'd ever mentioned that. (I suppose they hoped I would remember its name so they could track down when she left. I couldn't help.)

They asked about who shopped, who cooked, who paid the bills. I probably looked blank at all their questions. I mean, I knew Mum used to do the shopping. But after she fell down the wall that time, and Harris couldn't get her standing, not even after he'd calmed down, he had to do the shopping himself. He'd bring the things he fancied back in a box and dump it on the table. Sometimes he'd eat it, but a lot of the time he bought food for himself when he was out. He often came back smelling of curry or pizza. I never knew if he might want the things out of the box to eat himself so I left most of it, just to be safe. But I did know the things that Harris didn't like so much, so I fed Mum on those till she was able to hold the spoon herself again, without too much spilling. So how was I to know the answer to the questions that they asked? Who did the shopping and cooking? Everything was so mixed up.

I did my best, though. And after a while somebody brought in chips – brilliant hot chips with ketchup on a plate. Sue and Rob made a few jokes between them about how they'd invited a wolf to tea, and should have ordered double. But on the questions went. Some made

31

sense, even to me. And some seemed very odd, like wanting to know exactly what I remembered of the way Gem died, and how long it took. (I didn't know. I didn't count the days. I just remembered Harris kept on idly kicking at her twitching legs and saying, 'Oh, for God's sake, get on with it.')

All stuff like that. I didn't mind. They'd put me in a great big chair with cushions. Rob Reed was there. He'd made it clear that I would never, ever see Harris again unless I wanted to, and that was enough to make it the best day ever for me.

'So do you remember going to any school?'

'Mum said I went to one with little trucks. I think I remember that. You could have yellow or red, but every-one wanted the red ones.'

Sue asked, 'Did they have pedals, Eddie?'

I had to think for a while. Then I remembered. 'No. You pushed them with your feet.'

Sue turned to Rob. 'Nursery school, then? Or day care?'

Rob asked me, 'Nothing after that?'

'He didn't like it,' I told them. 'He told Mum people would get nosy if I was going in and out. He said he liked to keep his family to himself, and I was no one else's business.'

'Family?' Rob Reed leaned forward. 'Eddie, do you remember ever being with your mum and living with anyone else? Some other sort of dad? Sometime before?'

I shook my head.

'Your mother never talked of anyone?'

I didn't want to tell him that she'd stopped talking. So I just looked at the trainers they had given me. I really liked them. They were the sort the boys who rode their bikes around the flats wore all the time.

'Oh, well,' he said, 'I'm sure we'll find out something.' He looked at his watch. 'I think we might as well call it a day, unless you have some questions of your own.'

I only had one. 'Where's my mum?'

'Right now, she's busy seeing doctors,' Rob Reed said.

I felt a stab of panic. 'Is she ill?'

'Come on!' he chided. 'Think about those bruises. And her head must be sore. We think she needs a few days to recover, then she'll be more herself, and you can see her.'

'Is she in that hospital? Where you took me?'

'No, not in that one. In another one. Safe, well away from Harris.'

Somebody opened the door. I couldn't see a face but I heard what she said. 'Hey, Rob. Want to wind up for the day? The poor lad can't be older than seven.'

Rob Reed asked one last question. 'Is that right?'

I look back now, and find it really strange to have to say this. But out of all the scores of questions I was asked that day, and all the days that followed, that was the only one I couldn't even try to answer.

I had no idea.

Linda Radlett, Foster Carer

I didn't ask the boy questions. I simply settled him on the sofa alongside Rob and said, 'Well, you're a nice surprise. We were just saying, Alan here and I, that life was getting dull and what we'd like to see most in the world is a fresh face.'

He didn't know how to respond, so he sat tight, glancing at Alan from beneath that mop of hair he'd clearly hacked at himself. The nurse who bathed him must have had a go at tidying him up. But if there's one thing that I recognize from all the kids that come through here, it's the remains of a do-it-yourself haircut.

He didn't look too worried, though. And I'm not surprised at that. There's no way Alan and I look threatening. I will admit I have turned 'motherly looking' over the years, and Alan is pink, soft and bald. (One of our kids once said my husband looks like a walking sausage wearing a really tight belt. And, though the description still amuses me, it is so close to true I never bring it up.)

Alan asked Rob, 'Fancy a beer?' and Rob said, 'Sorry, can't,' then followed up almost at once with, 'Oh, God, why not? It's been a day and a half. But just the one, mind.'

'We've got alcohol-free.'

Rob looked much happier. 'That's just the ticket. Save my licence for another day.'

The boy's eyes were mostly down. But he was keeping tabs. Every few seconds he'd glance up, fast as a bird's peck, from beneath his fringe. He clearly wasn't sure what they were talking about, but he had that same look so many of the children who come to us keep on their faces. Blank, so they don't set anyone off. If they could make themselves invisible the poor mites would. And watchful, because they're used to trouble springing out of nothing and nowhere.

Be prepared.

Yet even that first night there was something unusual about his wariness. It seemed *intelligent* – more on the ball than most of the children we get who come from violent homes. Too many of the ones who have been lifted out of that particular sort of danger are so concerned with keeping a weather eye out for the next blow-up that they don't have a single brain cell left to use in more enriching ways. The rest of their mind is not just empty for their age, it's all but frozen.

Not this little guy. He sat there, cautious, vigilant; but he was *interested*. If he reminded me of anyone, it was Orlando, who was much the same age, and came to us while the police were tracking down his aunt and cousins after the crash that orphaned him instantly. Until that weekend, Orlando had obviously had the best of everything – a steady home, kind school, a host of hobbies and a lot of friends. And though he knew the worst, and kept on bursting into tears when he remembered, in between times he had that same outgoing, curious look as if he couldn't help but think, now-*this*-is-interesting about everything that went on under our roof, from the way Alan held his knife and fork to my recycling system, from how I swore when that cat next door got at the robin's nest to why no one had finished papering the downstairs lavatory.

We've done this job so long that most of them remind me of some other child. And Eddie was like Orlando. So I was very tempted to believe there had been good in his life. From what Rob said, it clearly wasn't that Bryce Harris chap I'd seen on television being led into court under a blanket. And somehow I was doubtful it was his mother, since the first officer to trawl the neighbouring flats for information reported back to Rob that Eddie's mum had been a fairly pitiful mess right from the start.

The boy was cooped up in that flat for years. Everyone who noticed him on the day the family moved in presumed that he lived somewhere else – off with some parent from a previous relationship, even in care. It never occurred to them that he was still in there. Had it not been for some good busybody who saw his face at the window and poked the Social Services into action, nobody would have known. He could have died in that flat, been buried in some ditch, and no one would have been any the wiser. You ask yourself, how can a child become invisible like that? But it is easy enough if, like Bryce Harris, you know how to do a moonlight flit, not letting your down-trodden partner leave any word behind, or take a single step towards a new life for herself and her young son.

I followed Rob out to his car. 'Do we even know his full *name*?'

'Not yet,' he said. 'There's someone going back tomorrow, to sort through the crap in the flat. They usually find something.'

'Can't you ask his mother?'

He made a face. 'Not sure what's happening there.'

'Nobody asked her when they took her out?'

'Linda,' he said, 'you've simply no idea what state that woman was in. She was just whimpering flesh. She's been that bastard's punchbag for three whole years. Frankly I doubt she knows her own name now, let alone his.'

'He didn't bring anything away with him? No cuddly toy? No blankie?'

I watched him looking shifty. Then he said, 'I didn't know if I should give it you.' He reached into the glove compartment and pulled out a grubby-looking book.

I turned it over to read the title. '*The Devil Ruled the Roost*?' I flicked it open. Dense print and narrow margins, with quite a few old-fashioned illustrations tucked under sheets of tissue. 'Oh, come on, Rob. This can't be his.'

He blushed. 'I found it propping up a table leg. But he did seem to want it.'

'I can't think why. The child can't possibly read at *this* level.'

'Linda, we don't even know if he can read full stop.'

I didn't hand it back. You never know. But mostly what I was thinking was that, given they'd had the mother and the child all day, they didn't seem to have got very far at all.

Eddie

I loved both of the Radletts from the start. They were the sort of people that Mr Perkins visited. I could imagine him coming through their front door and asking them, 'Why is the hall painted red?' or 'Where did you get this line of wooden elephants on the shelf?'

Linda called me into the kitchen and sat me on a stool. I watched her cut things up and put them into bowls. 'Have you done any cooking, Eddie?'

I shook my head.

She showed me how to use the cheese grater, and gave me a lump to start on. I made a bit of a mess. It was a whole lot harder than I thought to hold things steady on the wooden board. But Linda didn't mind. She just brushed all the scattered shreds of cheese over the edge of the table into her hand and sprinkled them on top of her big oval dish. Then she went over to a drawer and pulled out some knives and forks and spoons. 'Know how to set a table?'

Of course I didn't, so she showed me how, saying, 'You'll pick it up.'

'Will I be staying here, then?'

She stopped what she was doing and turned to face me. 'Remember what Rob said? That we're not sure of anything yet, not till we know a little more about you. But you will certainly be here tonight, and probably for several days. And maybe even longer than that, if we get on together.' She rubbed her hand over my hair and smiled. 'Long enough to get you a haircut, anyhow.'

'Another haircut,' I corrected her.

She gave me an odd look. Then she went back to putting the bowls and plates in place, and showing me which chair I was to sit on. 'Rob reckons you'll have ruined your appetite with all those chips. But never mind. Just have a go.'

She called to Alan and we started to eat. I wasn't sure about the food. I wasn't used to lettuce or tomato, and all that stuff. I ate the cheesy topping – not just because I was the one to grate it. I love cheese. This had a funny taste, and it felt different in my mouth from any I had eaten before. But I still loved it.

While I was eating, they were talking the whole time, the two of them. Not to me, but to each other. He chatted about someone he'd met that morning in the supermarket, and how she seemed to be doing really well after the death of her husband. And Linda talked about a phone call she had had from someone called Alice. They didn't talk about me, and they didn't really talk to me, except that Alan kept saying, 'If you're not eating that,

I'll have it, if you don't mind,' and Linda told me, 'Alice is one of our daughters. She's grown up now.'

I think that they were pleased at how much cheese I ate. Then Linda brought out ice cream. Ice cream was something I knew all about, because of Mr Perkins. 'Ice cream is made from eggs and cream and then a flavouring that can be anything – anything at all,' I told them. 'Even a combination like, for example, coffee and toffee pecan.'

They did try not to stare, but you could tell they thought that what I'd said was really weird. So when Alan asked me, 'What's *your* favourite, then?' I kept my head down and I didn't answer. I wasn't quite sure what he meant. I'd only ever seen ice cream on television. And I don't think I even knew what 'flavouring' meant.

The moment passed and they went back to talking about Alice's new job. I ate the ice cream. Then I ate some more. Then Linda said, 'I'll let you skip the bath, since Rob says that you had one at the hospital.'

I wasn't sure why she said that. Back then, I didn't know about routines and such. But I could see she was expecting me to get up and follow her, so I did. We went upstairs. She showed me where she and Alan slept. 'You just knock and come in if you need anything. Promise?' She pulled pyjamas out of a pile on a shelf, and I remember being really surprised at how tidy everything in the cupboard was – even the flannels were folded. She pushed me in the bathroom and gave me a toothbrush and a lesson in how to brush my teeth. (It was the same way Mr Perkins said, but using a brush with bristles that stood up made it feel different.)

Then she turned down the light till it was just a glow and sat on my bed.

'Story?'

'Yes, please.'

So she read one or two. I don't think I was listening. I was just looking around the room. I felt so high up in that bed, and worried that I might fall out. And I was wondering if my mother had had a bath as well, and if the nurses in the hospital had a cupboard with pyjamas and a toothbrush.

'Do you think my mum's all right?'

She broke off reading the book and leaned her face down close to mine. 'You know she's in the hospital. And you know she's safe there. No one can get at her. So we'll just cross our fingers and hope your mum's already start-ing to feel better.'

I crossed my fingers hard.

'And no one can get at you, either,' she told me. 'You are just as safe here. We lock the doors really well at night. So you sleep sound. And we'll start thinking about every-thing else tomorrow morning, shall we?'

I must have nodded.

'Kiss?'

I don't know why I shook my head. I used to like it when Mum hugged and kissed me. But she turned at the door and blew a kiss from there. (I didn't understand what she was doing till the next night, when she did it again.)

She left the door half-open. I slid out of bed and listened through the gap. Linda was going into the kitchen. Before the door closed behind her, she said, 'Alan, remind me to phone the dentist tomorrow. Did you *see* his mouth?'

I wasn't scared. I'd visited the dentist with Mr Perkins. If I felt anything, it was excitement. I shut the door, then pulled the downie off the bed to heap it in the corner. It was a whole lot puffier than the blankets I had shared with Gem. But still I couldn't sleep for a long time.

PC Martin Tallentire

For all the fuss in the papers, we knew we couldn't keep Bryce Harris locked up for long. He'd barely touched the boy. And when I phoned the hospital to see if I could get to see the mother, they told me that they'd given her some knock-out drops, and she'd be no use for a day or two.

Or even then, I thought, if I know her sort. We see them often enough, these women who've been eased away from all their friends and family, their jobs, and any-one who might support them in the business of leaving a thug. It happens in all sorts of families. Sometimes it's simple intimidation: threats, bashings and the like. In others, the way it works can be more subtle. Everyone's friends and relations get up their noses now and again. Most people let it be. They just back off until they feel a whole lot less annoyed, then they pick up the threads. But when one of these grim control freaks gets involved, you're in big trouble. You are so much easier meat if you've no one to turn to, no one to say to you, 'Excuse me? He did *what*?' 'He hit you *where*?' 'Christ, I would not put up with that – not for a single moment!'

And so the bully gradually and deliberately pushes all of these people out of your life. Your mother: 'The old cow hates me! I can tell! You're going to have to choose. It's me or her!' Your sister. 'She's a bitch! Look how she didn't even speak to me when she was round here last time. This is my house and I don't want her here!' Your friends are easily frozen out. Even the girlfriend you have known for years stops calling for a while because her child's sick, or she's distracted or depressed, and in the bully steps. 'She can't be much of a friend.' 'I never mentioned it, but you should hear the things she says about you behind your back.' On it goes. 'Well, you can visit your Aunt Sue, but I'm not taking you. I'll need the car for work. You'll have to get to Scotland on the bus.'

Throw in the sulks and tempers, and the occasional stray fist let loose to put you right ('That was *your* fault, that was. You were provoking me!') and keeping in touch with anyone you liked or loved becomes not worth the effort. Your friends begin to take the hint, and drop away. Your family try to tell you a few home truths about your choice of partner, and that's more grist to the bully's mill. ('See? They've had a down on me right from the start!') And soon your world is him, and only him. And after that you gradually begin to see the whole boiling around you through his eyes because you're so run down, and on your own, and standing up for yourself is so much harder than not arguing back. And if that makes you just a bag of worthless shite, because he tells you so, then you believe it. Add a few hard thumps and beatings, and it can take no time at all to turn an upright cheerful person into the sort of snivelling muppet that we police officers bail out time and again.

So best of luck to Mrs Bryce Harris, or whoever she was, with her long hospital sleep. Better off out of it, since all the woman has to wake to now is a child taken into care and one big mess.

But it was up to me to find out all the details. So while we had Bryce Harris under lock and key on suspicion of grievous bodily harm, I went back to the flat. One of our locks was on the damaged door to keep the neighbours out. In I went, hammering open windows as I walked through because of the stink. I was quite glad to see the dog was gone. I reckoned I owed someone from the council offices a pint for that. Now it was my job to go through the place with a fine-tooth comb, looking for anything that might give rise to tracking down the past.

I was allowed to shift things about. They'd already taken all the photographs that one or two of those buffoons in Social Services might need to see a second time if they went all soft-headed, and talked of sending the child 'home'. I would have thought the bruises on the mother's legs would be enough. But Martha had photographed all around the flat as well. ('Got some quite arty ones of all that dog poo.')

I spent an hour or so opening drawers. Anything that was useless – the special offers, packs of cards, catalogues, porn – I threw in a pile on the floor. I kept the bills because you can track down a host of aliases and previous addresses from some of those. Crushed in a drawer were several anonymous letters about the noise the dog made all the time, and one warning Harris that if he didn't cough up what he owed, he'd get a visitor he didn't want. That too was left unsigned. The place was knee-deep in receipts, some three or four years old. Fags, beer and groceries mainly. I must say, that surprised me. I would have had Bryce Harris down for the sort that lets the receipts for anything he hasn't shoplifted drop in the street because he can't be arsed to stuff them in his pockets.

Then I went through the big cupboard in the bedroom, tossing the bottles behind me onto the bed so I could get right to the back. Christ, there were some horrors in there, but I pressed on. I found a discount card to some toddlers' soft playcentre called Hurlabout.

(Result! *Name of child:* Edward Taylor.) I found a hair-dresser's card tucked in a tampon box. A Cut Above. The salon's address was in Sunderland. No time or date, but we were definitely getting somewhere. I found a first birthday card from somebody who'd signed herself Nana, but with so doddery a hand I reckoned she was probably out of it by now, all these years later. A postmark might usefully have pinned down Eddie's year of birth, but the envelope was gone.

Then, at the back, I found the tidy little tower of unmarked tapes, with an old shirt draped over. I counted eleven of them, and hauled them out because I hoped we might get Harris for distributing porn – though it was most unlikely that any charge would stick, videotapes dating back almost to the days when showing a little bit of you-know-what was seen as daring. Most of the people in these blocks are skint, but if there's one thing they spend money on, it's fancy electronics. The only people with machines that could still play these things were all those middle-class old folk on the other side of town, hoarding their old boxed sets of *The Forsyte Saga* and *I, Claudius.*

Still, any chance to get that bastard under lock and key was worth the effort, so I heaved the tapes into my evidence box and kept on, poking through the cupboards till even the rubber gloves I wore disgusted me. The kitchen was a greasy pit. Revolting. I couldn't even face the garbage can. I swear if Eddie's birth certificate had

46

been on top of that, in a clean plastic bag, I wouldn't have picked it out.

Last came the bathroom. There was a stash of drugs inside the cistern, as there so often is. Good. One more possible charge. I didn't bother with the mess of slimy bottles, or the sodden towels. I just kicked them aside to check that there was nothing underneath except more filth and mess. I broke the catch to push the window open and check the outside sill for yet more drugs, but all there was out there was heaps and heaps of ancient bird shit.

I picked my box up and walked out. When I got in the street the fresh air hit me in the face.

That poor boy had lived in that foul stink for four whole years. And no one had noticed. Christ alive! Sometimes I hate this country.

Linda Radlett, Foster Carer

I have to say that he was one of the easiest boys we've ever had. More of them than you'd think are good as gold – often from gratitude at feeling safe. But they still worry you with their haunted eyes and inability to concentrate, as if the only thing inside their heads is trying not to upset you.

Eddie was different. The way he responded was extraordinary for a child who'd come from a place like that. On the very first morning, Alan said to him, 'You're doing a fine imitation of a concrete mixer, chomping away on that egg with your mouth wide open.'

'I've seen a concrete mixer,' he said. 'On telly.' And you could almost watch him processing the memory to work out what it was that Alan had meant. And then he giggled with delight and shut his mouth! And after that, we only had to turn to one another and say, 'Is someone round this table mixing concrete?' and he'd clamp his lips together. He learned fast.

The bed-wetting too. Obviously for the first couple of nights we thought it might just stem from tension and exhaustion. But soon it was obvious that it was a regular thing, so I persuaded Eddie to settle for a bed protector over the heap of folded blankets on the floor that he felt safer on, scared of the 'too high' bed. But then, as soon as we got into the routine of leading him through for a pee before we turned in ourselves, hey presto! He was practically dry.

And he asked questions all the time. Intelligent questions. 'Why do you do it *that* way?' 'Why do you keep it *there*?' 'How does it *work*?' It was a little like having a seven-year-old toddler trailing after us.

And there were odder questions too. 'What's a blood family, Linda?'

That stopped me in my tracks. I bustled round a bit, pouring my coffee. And then I ran my arm round his thin body to pull him close. 'Have you heard someone saying it?'

48

He nodded.

'Can you tell me who that was?'

'Not sure,' he told me anxiously. 'Might have been Rob. Or Sue.'

'Oh, right!' Well, that was a relief. He'd clearly had the little speech I'd heard some social workers give a dozen times. So I knew what to say. 'Most babies are born into families, Eddie. Some people call them "blood families" because the baby's made out of the same sort of skin and bone and blood and stuff as their mum and dad.'

'They're not covered in blood.'

'No. They're *not* covered in blood.' I gave him a moment to digest this before pointing to the raised veins on my hand. 'See those wriggly blue lines? That's all my blood rushing around my body, doing its job.'

'It's blue?'

'Not really. Yes, the lines look blue, but if I cut myself, it would bleed red.' I took his soft little paw. 'And you've got blood in there too. It's just your skin's so fresh and young that we can't see it going round.'

I let him leave his hand beside my battered old one for a while, and then I said, 'The blood in me is the same sort my mum and dad had. And the blood in you is like your mum and dad's. That's why some people call your mum and dad and brothers and sisters your "blood family".' I pulled him closer. 'And mostly families work well and babies grow up there. But sometimes things go wrong, like they did for you, and then people like Rob and Sue

49

decide it would be better if you come to stay with people like us. Just for a while.'

I felt him stiffen at those last few words, so said it yet again. 'But you will never, ever go back to Harris.'

'You *promise?*'

'I already did. About a hundred times.'

'Not a *hundred*,' he rebuked me. 'Not nearly a *hundred*. More like' – he counted on his fingers - 'nearly *ten?*'

Oh, he was bright enough.

He didn't go to school at first. I reckoned if we kept him home, I could teach him to read a little quicker, one to one. (I used to be a teacher.) And so we started off with all my old staged readers. He knew the names of the letters, but still had to learn the phonic way of saying them. Then we were off. I bribed him along with little things he needed anyway. (I'd never seen a child with less in his Personal Box, and I was not sure when he would move on.) But after a while, as he began to get his confidence, the tiny treasures that I handed out were less important. He was on it in a flash, reading road signs to me whenever we went out, and almost incapable of pushing a shopping trolley past a sign without proudly reading it aloud to anyone around.

That supermarket. The first time we went, his mouth dropped open and he followed me around quite mesmerized, like a small zombie. On an aisle end where they sell stuff off really cheap, close to the date stamp, he whispered excitedly, 'I know them! We ate them a lot!'

Once we were home and unpacked, I asked him what it was he'd liked so much about the place. First he said that it was the great long lights. Then that it was 'so *huge*'. Then, 'So much stuff, but all in *places*.' In the end I reckoned what struck him so forcibly was the sheer *order* of the shop. And after that, neither Alan nor I could do the shortest supermarket run without him begging, 'Can *I* come?'

I took him to the dentist, thinking that things were far worse than they were. Angela said to him, 'Open your mouth for me, pet,' and I expected to hear the usual cascade of clicks on the assistant's keyboard as she flagged up each rotten stump and cavity – the usual stuff.

But, no. 'Well,' Angela said when they were finished. 'It's not too good. But let's be fair, it isn't that bad either. We can deal with that.'

His eyes were wide. I'd no idea what her words meant to him, but she says that her tack of treating all the children like adults and all the adults like children has worked so far, so she keeps to it, even with my strange brood.

She turned to me. 'Most of that rather weird-looking mess is normal. Things falling out and others growing in. There are some cavities I'll fill next week. But' – here she smiled at Eddie – '*someone* around here has clearly been looking after his gums and using his toothbrush. So, well done you.'

Eddie looked pleased. He lapped up praise. It made

him almost radiant. 'I didn't always use the toothbrush,' he confessed to me on the drive home. 'But Mr Perkins took us to see a dentist and he told us that, in an emergency, like if we went camping and forgot to pack it, we can do a pretty good job using a finger.'

By then I had become accustomed to what Alan had begun to call 'The Wit and Wisdom of Mr P'.

After a couple of weeks, I dared take Eddie swimming. He'd never been, and one of my jobs is to ease these children into normal life. They have to know the things the others know, or there's no hope of ever making and keeping friends. So I did what I usually do – borrowed a smaller child to give us an excuse for keeping to the toddler pool.

We took Marie, from next door. She's only two years old, but she is sturdy. And watching Marie gave him confidence. Again, you could see Eddie thinking, 'If *she's* OK . . .' And after he had sat for a while scrunched in a ball on the side, getting used to the echoing noise and the splashing, and the sheer height of the glassed roof, he dared to slide his feet into the water and stand up. I think he was astonished it only came halfway up to his knees. He paddled further down the slope, survived his first splashed drops from two more toddlers having a water fight, and made it over to me.

Marie reached out for him, but it turned out to be more of a push than a clutch. He staggered backwards, losing his balance in the shallow water enough to have to sit down. But once he realized that the water still came up no deeper than a bath, he was away. Before we left, even on that first day, Eddie was spending most of his time on his stomach, ferrying himself across the baby pool with his hands, pretending to swim.

I didn't know how long we'd have him. Sometimes that can depend on when the child sees a psychologist. And if there's any possibility of giving evidence in court, that often gets delayed in case the defence starts arguing that ideas have been put in the child's mind. So I was really waiting for Rob to let me know. I'd used the standard grant to take him shopping for clothes. He was entranced. Usually we encourage them to make their own choices, but that didn't work with Eddie. He only wanted things like Thomas the Tank Engine shirts, and other baby stuff that would have had him shredded at the local primary school. He hadn't learned that pink is social death for boys. I had to be quite firm.

So in the end we compromised with suitable stuff for daytime, but Thomas pyjamas. He loved the things so much that I went back the following week to get another pair. But even in the largest size, they were too short. 'You're soft, you are,' said Alan, when he saw me sewing extra strips onto the legs and sleeves to lengthen them.

But I'd have sold my soul for Eddie. I had fallen in love.

(They warn you about that when you sign on.)

Eddie

The first time Linda mentioned it, we were sitting at the table, the way we did every day. Her hand had closed round mine to make sure I was holding the pencil the way she said was best – 'No, Eddie. Like *that*. And now make me a capital S, just like a lovely curled snake. Yes, that's right! Perfect!'

I was so happy. And then she suddenly made her voice go all casual, and out it came. 'By the way, I was thinking about your mum last night. The bruises on her leg must have gone now. Maybe she's feeling better. Would you like me to talk to Rob about fixing up a visit?'

I didn't trust myself to answer so I shook my head.

She kept on, trying to persuade me. 'She'd probably be really pleased to see how well your writing's coming on.'

I knew that Linda didn't really think that. I knew what they all thought because I listened all the time. Up on the landing. At doors. I acted good. I *was* good. But I still had two ears that worked, and wasn't stupid. From the day of that first hammering on the door, I'd overheard all sorts of things that people said about my mum, whispering in corridors or talking quietly on phones – 'in no fit state to defend the child', 'probably too scared to testify', 'under that bastard's thumb' – until I knew full well that everyone thought that she was useless. *Useless.*

But I could remember back when we played the first tape. I know when Harris slammed out, Mum was a little nervous. There was a tremble in her voice when she said, 'Never mind! Moving house makes people ratty. When he comes back, he'll probably be in a better temper.' She rubbed the red mark round the wrist he'd held too tightly and too long. She told me it was called a Chinese Burn, and that the girls in her class when she was at school gave them to one another. And then she tried to laugh, and said, 'We'll make some cocoa, and then see what's on those old tapes in the corner. Maybe there's a film.'

She slid one in the old machine the other people hadn't bothered to take away with them. ('Leaving their crap!' said Harris.) We waited, then the music for the song came on, and Mr Perkins came through the bright red door, took off his jacket and began to sing. And I remember Mum looking at him, then saying, 'Perfect. All I'm bloody fit for!' and giving this weird little laugh. And then she squeezed me – almost too tightly, like a giant Chinese Burn, and I was in her lap, all warm and comfy.

But she hadn't been like that for ages and ages and ages. So I didn't want to go and see her. Even if the bruises had gone.

Linda Radlett, Foster Carer

He picked things up so quickly that it was easy to forget his childhood had been so strange. But every now and again he'd freeze, or look uncertain about the most straightforward thing, and we'd be reminded that, however sensible and caring his babyhood might have been, everything had been sent off track in recent years.

Take mirrors. Mirrors fascinated Eddie. He stopped in front of them the way that other children do when they are at a fair, and find themselves facing distorting glass. 'Look, Mum! I'm fat as a barrel!' 'See, Dad! I am the rubber boy!'

Eddie just stared. Most times, I think, he took himself at first simply for some other child his age passing a window. His double-takes stemmed more from simple spatial puzzlement – how can someone be walking *there*? – than recognition of his own reflection. As soon as he had clocked it was himself that he was looking at, he'd stop and stare – gaze at himself in wonder. 'Is this me?' Of course we realized at once that, since he was too young to notice, he had never seen himself. Still, Alan and I couldn't work out quite what it was that so astonished him. Was he surprised he looked so tall? So clean? So grave? Did he not realize children looked like that?

Because he'd pass for normal almost anywhere. He was what an American I knew used to call 'biddable'. Lord knows, we have had kids through here who've acted out so badly that we've recoiled from taking them anywhere in public. We have had children who've been, to use the jargon, 'challenging in the extreme'.

Eddie was not like that.

It was as if he knew a lot of all this social stuff already, and simply hadn't had the chance to practise it. And then we realized who we had to thank for that. Isn't life strange? A quarter of the way across the world, in Canada, and thirty years ago, some sweet old fellow in a cardigan called Mr Perkins makes a series of telly programmes for children. Someone else bothers to record them, but doesn't throw them out. And Edward James Taylor is saved for life. If this sort of thing could only happen a good deal more often, I might be able to believe in God.

Alan and I tried not to ask the boy too many questions. But Rob did. One of the bones I'd pick with Social Services is that they can be too much like our dentist, treating small fry like adults where sometimes I believe it's best for people like ourselves, who have been parents a long while, to use our intuition about what should be said, or what should happen next.

Rob came a lot, sometimes just for a chat with Eddie, sometimes with news. 'Guess what I've just found out. It seems you have a great-grandmother.'

Eddie looked baffled.

I heard the sofa sigh from Rob's weight as he dropped on it. 'That's your mother's own granny. She's really old now, but she sends her love.' Wearily he shook his head. 'Maybe one day I'll drive you up to visit her. Would you like that?'

'Up?'

I wondered if Eddie had a vision of this great-grand-mother up somewhere in a cloud, or on a star.

'On Tyneside,' Rob said. 'Quite a long way away.' You could tell he was dreading the drive. We sat in silence for a moment or two, and then, as if his mind was drifting far away, Rob added, 'Her feet are terrible, she says. Like sponges.'

I watched poor Eddie trying to imagine this. 'Sponges?'

'Never mind that,' said Rob – a little irritably, I thought, considering that it was he himself who'd brought the matter up. 'The other news is that the flat you used to live in has now been re-let.'

'Rob!' I protested. (I mean, a home's a home, however grim it's been.)

'He has to *know*,' Rob muttered defensively.

Re-let? What sort of language is that for someone of Eddie's age? 'What Rob is *saying*,' I explained, 'is that the flats where you lived belong to something called a Housing Association. And since Harris definitely won't be going back, they have decided to clear out all his stuff, paint the place till it looks new, and put another family in there.'

'So will I live with *them*?'

At last, Rob was ashamed. I think he must have panicked momentarily because he said the worst thing he could say. 'Of course not. You'll be staying here with Linda and Alan.'

Eddie was on it in a flash. 'For *ever*?'

Rob looked so miserable I couldn't even give him my

see-what-you've-done-now look. I had to rescue him, so I ticked Eddie off. 'Come along, Eddie. You know better than that. Alan and I have told you plenty of times that we only look after children for a little while, till Rob here and the people he works with find them something that will work better.'

(I won't use their expression, 'a for ever family'. It is such *bollocks*.)

I left the two of them together for a while. When I came back, Rob was just leaving. I made some excuse to send Eddie down to Alan in the shed, and turned to Rob.

'A great-granny, eh? But no one who could take the boy? No grandmother on that side?'

'The police tracked down some hairdresser in Tynemouth who knew the family. She said the grandmother died some years ago.'

'No father hiding anywhere in the woodwork?'

He shook his head. 'My money is on Harris. It seems the mum was managing fine till he showed up. My guess is that it wasn't for the first time.'

'I hope no one is going to rush to tell poor Eddie *that*.' I sighed. 'So. One great-granny. No future there, I suppose?'

'No,' Rob agreed. 'She's bed-bound in a home. The staff aren't even sure she was on top of what they told her.' He glanced around to check that Eddie hadn't crept back to eavesdrop. 'I have some better news, though. There won't be a court case.'

'His mum won't testify?'

'She's quite unfit.'

'What about a video link?'

He leaned towards me. 'Linda, she's *hopeless*. Harris could come into court swinging a rusty mace, and any jury would still hesitate to convict. None of the neighbours will say a thing. And Lucy Taylor's such a mess in the head it's hard to imagine that she wasn't always some sort of basket case.'

'So is he going to get away with it?'

'Of course not,' Rob said hotly. 'They're nailing him for drugs, and common assault and stolen goods, and animal cruelty and numerous shenanigans inside that club, and God knows what else. They've rustled up a list an arm's length long.'

'You know as well as I do that, without bodily harm or kidnapping, the man will be out within months.'

'I know.' He studied the ends of his fingers. 'He was a crafty sod, to take care to lay off the child. But, on the bright side, Eddie can see someone now.'

He meant a therapist, though in my experience with damaged children, that isn't always a bright side. 'Anyone in particular?'

He looked embarrassed. 'I thought it might be Eleanor Holdenbach? Sometime next month?'

Eleanor Holdenbach. It could have been a whole lot worse. And I was just relieved it wasn't Otto Weeks. Otto's so young he still has hobby horses. Most of the rest have worked for the council long enough to realize the job is just to tidy up what chunks of the child are left and brush as many of the splinters as they can out of sight, out of mind. Otto's so full of beans he still believes that you can focus on exactly what went wrong, and make the poor little buggers whole again.

So, 'Eleanor,' I said. 'Next month.'

Lewis Tanner, Investigations Department Technician

We ran the tapes Martin brought in. God, that was a laugh. There we were, all of the other screens slopping over with what my grandmother calls 'the bits no one should see in places they shouldn't go'. And there, in the corner, on the old video player, this middle-aged goody-goody in a cardigan is asking some other codger how to make ice cream.

We sat and roared. I gave Martin a call, but he insisted that we did a thorough job and played every tape through. And he is right that all too often underneath this stuff, you catch a glimpse of something that sickens you so much you want to pack in the whole caboodle – move to some other section where you don't feel, when you go home at night, that you'd prefer a single bed.

Don't tell my wife I said that!

Anyhow, we followed orders. *Jawohl, mein Kommandant!*

For six days in a row, we slid in these old tapes. There were five programmes on each. We got to know the songs. The two of us began to sing each time the show began.

> *'Happy days, and happy ways*
> *I hope you know how glad I am*
> *To see you here with me today*
> *We're going to have great fun.'*

We even sang it in the canteen once. (Fat Terry said he thought it sounded rather familiar, but he's a hundred years old.) Then we went back to shove in the next tape. This was the visit to the fire station. (The officer was tactful. He didn't mention that they call dead bodies 'crispies'.) Then came how plasticine is made. How people engrave on glass. We learned it all. It was a very educational week.

And, as Gurdeep said, not one wet knob or fanny from start to finish. That made a pleasant change.

Eddie

I thought that Rob had already asked me every question on earth. And Sue had often come along as well, sometimes in uniform, and sometimes not. They'd kept it up between them, tiptoeing around Linda and Alan ('We'll

be all right in here, will we? Out from under your feet?').
They'd tried to keep it light, cheering me up along the
way with biscuits, and offers to take me along to the playground. ('All of us need a breath of fresh air. Fancy a kick
about?')

But they'd kept at it. 'Eddie, what did you *do* all day?
How did you pass the time?' 'Did you ever have the little
bed? Or did you always sleep along with Gem on that
blanket?' I told them that the little bed was mine until
one day he'd tipped me out of it, saying he needed the
room to store a few boxes he'd brought home, and Rob
said, more into Sue's tiny silver recording machine than
to me, 'To clarify, Eddie, can you tell us who you mean
by "he"?'

I couldn't work out what he was talking about, so I'd
kept quiet. I mean, he *knew* that I meant Harris. Why was
he asking?

And I remember Rob had tried again. 'What did you
call him, when you spoke to him?'

I probably looked blank. I'd never called him anything.

Sue tried. 'What did your mum call him?'

She hadn't, much. But still I said it, just to keep them
off me. 'Bryce.'

'So did you call him Bryce as well?'

They waited. Maybe they were thinking that I was
trying to remember.

'Well, did you call him Dad?' persisted Sue.

'No.'

'Harris?' She tried to hide it, but she was watching me as if she thought I was pretending to be thick. 'Or Mr Harris, even?'

'I never called him anything.'

'What if you wanted to call him over to look at something?'

Did I look frightened at the very idea? Who'd want him looking? I found a ladybird once, and he pulled her legs off, one by one, in front of my face. Then, holding me tight between his knees so I couldn't get away, he crushed her tiny body slowly between his big fat thumbs. But in the end I couldn't see for crying anyway. So I won there.

'Right, then,' I do remember Sue saying very firmly into the machine. 'For now, we're going to refer to Edward Taylor's mother's partner as "Harris" on this tape.'

And on we'd gone. 'What did you eat? Did you have to tell them when you were hungry, or did they feed you anyway?' 'Who gave you food? Was it hot or cold?' 'Were you allowed to take food out of the cupboards by yourself or did you have to ask?'

Next time, they'd take another tack. I look back now and I can hardly believe that I had no idea what they were fishing for, with some of their questions. 'Eddie, I must ask, did you see anyone apart from Harris and your mum? Did he have mates in ever?' 'Eddie, did Harris ever hit you?' 'Where on your body?' 'How often, Ed – can you tell me?' 'How hard? I know it isn't easy to explain, but' – Rob slapped a hand on his own thigh – '*this* hard?

Or was it harder, more like this?' His hairy hand came down with such a thwack he made himself yelp.

After we'd giggled at that, it was Sue's turn to lean forward. 'Did your mum ever try to stop him hitting you?'

I tried so hard to hide the answer. But they were waiting. *Waiting*, just like Harris did.

Maybe I panicked. Anyhow, I must have nodded.

'So what happened then?'

And when they'd finally dragged that answer out of me, and Rob had held me tight, and I'd stopped sobbing, he'd said, 'Sorry, Eddie! God, I am so *sorry*! I had no *idea*!' And I looked across at Sue and she was scarlet in the face and scrabbling on the carpet on her hands and knees, picking up hundreds of tiny bits of grey foam rubber.

I hadn't meant to rip that cushion into shreds. I didn't realize I'd been clinging on to it so tightly. 'We will tell Linda it was not your fault that it got torn,' Rob promised me. And he made sure he did, as they were leaving. He even called me back so I could hear.

Linda looked down at the carpet, which was still speckled grey around my chair. 'Never you mind. We've had *far* worse than that.'

I couldn't understand what she was saying. What, I was worried, could be *worse* than what Harris did to Mum that time she tried to stop him?

That was the end, that day. But Sue and Rob came back again, and I remember being mystified at how some of the very same questions got asked over and over. I couldn't understand why. It felt to me, back then, as if Mr Perkins had asked one of the people we visited, 'Do the pancakes you're tossing ever end up on the floor by mistake?' and then, after she'd answered, kept asking the question again, but just a different way. I do remember worrying that they hadn't listened, or they hadn't believed my answers. Why else would they ask things like, 'Was Harris ever nice to you?' when they knew that he wasn't? Or, 'Did he ever come home with presents or promise you special things?' or, 'Did he or any of his friends ever put their arms around you or hug you – anything like that?' I had already *told* them that no one ever came, and Harris didn't touch me – no, never laid a hand on me, so long as I was crouched down quietly against that wall, gripping my legs so tightly to keep myself steady that I made bruises on myself, trying to stay safe by keeping what Harris called my 'dirty little pink snout' well out of it.

Being as good as gold so he wouldn't get ratty.

Charlotte Next Door

Linda came round some days to borrow my baby sister. It was usually for swimming, but after their new boy came, sometimes it was for her to go next door and sit with him in their sandpit. (Dad dug ours over after I stopped playing in it. Marie came years after me. She was a big surprise.)

Linda and Alan keep their old sandpit covered so the cats can't mess in it. Marie really likes it. I thought at first their new boy would be only two years old, like her. But then I saw him. He was nearly as old as me! And he was wearing Thomas the Tank Engine pyjamas. I didn't want to play with him when I saw that, and nobody suggested it. I don't know why.

I don't know either why the boy – his name was Eddie – would want to sit next to Marie, mucking about with sand. He did, though. She would crawl about, grabbing the spades and shovels, and bashing the top of buckets. He just sat jammed against the edge, scooping up handfuls of sand and watching it trickle away between his fingers. Over and over. Whenever Marie got upset because she couldn't see her favourite yellow scraper, he'd push it back in view. And sometimes, when she was chattering her nonsense, he'd nod as if he might be listening.

He didn't talk, though – except to say to Marie things like, 'There it is,' and, 'Over *there*.'

I watched quite often. Usually Alan was gardening some-where near, pretending not to keep an eye on things.

I asked Linda once, when I'd been sent round there to tell them that it was our tea time, 'Why do you put him in there with a *baby*?'

She looked at me. I could tell that she was going to make up some excuse. But then she didn't.

'I think he finds it soothing,' she told me. 'And some days, when he's had his visitors, it calms him down.'

I knew who she meant by 'his visitors'. She meant the dumpy man and the smart lady they called Sue.

Eddie

You cannot say I wasn't used to questions. But *Eleanor*. She had braids wrapped around her head, grey hair and dangly necklaces. Her spectacles hung round her neck when they weren't on her nose. I couldn't stand her – well, not *her* exactly, more the way she made me feel, because that awful waiting that we always did reminded me of being near to Harris. It made my heart thump, knowing that she'd be saying something any moment, but not knowing what or when. I'd try so hard to keep still, then I'd look in my lap to see my hands squirm. Or I would notice red and realize I'd gnawed a fingernail so far down that it was bleeding again.

She wasn't horrid. It was simply horrid being there, feeling like something she was studying. She'd sit me in the chair, give me a good long look, and then she'd say, 'Today, I thought that we might talk about—' And it would be this or that, and all those horrible long pauses after I'd done my best. And it was such a *cheat* because Linda and Alan had told me so often when I'd woken at night, 'Those days are *gone*. They are all over now.'

And here was Eleanor, just going on about it all, over and over and over. 'How did that make you feel?' 'Did you feel scared, Eddie?' 'Perhaps you felt very sad.' 'You probably felt—'

Linda would bring me home. I'd beg her, 'Read me a story!' and she would pull out *Frog and Toad*, or *Up the Faraway Tree*, or *The Smugglers' Secret*. Anything that wasn't to do with me and how I felt. I loved the way even the words on the page began to make sense. More and more often, Linda would drop her finger to the page and say, 'You read this line,' and I would find that I could do it. 'No!' 'Stop!' or 'Frog said, "Yes, Toad."'

I read it properly, as well. She said I put expression into it right from the start. I knew how to do that because Mr Perkins often read to us. Never a story, though. We'd come back from the day's visit and he'd say, 'Now that reminds me of a poem I learned at school when I was around your age.' He'd go to his yellow book shelf with the talking bookends, and run his finger along until one of the bookends squealed, 'That's right! That's the right book!' He'd prise it out, flick through the pages and read us a line or two. And he would always make it sound as if it *mattered*.

So even if I was just reading something simple like, '"Yes, Toad," said Frog,' I put my heart in it. And soon I found that Linda was pointing at the page for me to read not just a few odd words, but a whole sentence. It would be something like, 'I won't go there!' or, 'He is a fool!' or, 'You go home right now!' And after that, I just took off.

(Well, that's what Linda said.) And almost all of it was suddenly easy-peasy.

I could read.

And then, I don't know why, I wanted to tell Mum. I knew that Linda would be very surprised. She had kept asking and I'd kept shrugging my shoulders and saying nothing. So after I changed my mind, there was a bit of a silence. Then Linda asked me, 'Do you really want to go? Or is this Eleanor's idea?'

'I want to go.'

She squeezed my hand and said, 'All right. I'll talk to Rob. He'll probably be the one to take you.'

I overheard the phone call. I made sure I did. I played the usual trick of thumping around my bedroom, then crept out onto the landing.

'Rob, is this such a good idea? He's been so settled . . . Yes, I know. But does it have to be now, when he is doing so well? . . . No, you're wrong there. I don't believe he thinks that any more . . . Oh, God! You social workers and your bloody *guidelines*. What about *Eddie*?'

Eleanor Holdenbach, Child Psychologist

I'd seen the headlines, of course. WILD CHILD. OUR TINIEST SHUT-IN. BLUEBEARD BRUTALITY. MONSTER!!! The usual mix of noisy hysteria and sentimental wallowing.

70

Every front page featured that grainy photo of the boy blinking so fiercely as he shuffled into the light. And, just like everyone else, I'd seen the television footage of Bryce Harris's hand slipping out under the blanket covering his head to flip the bird at the baying crowd.

I never for a moment thought the child would come to me. I naturally assumed that this would be the sort of court case – kidnapping, false imprisonment, grievous bodily harm – that meant that Eddie would have to give evidence. Don't ask me the ins and outs of how Harris wriggled out of facing such obvious charges. I know it was something to do with the fact that young children are seen as unreliable witnesses. And it did certainly seem odd that this man should have had the self-control to keep his hands off the boy while he was beating up the mother.

Which led to the next problem for the police, for Eddie's mother was deemed to be incapable of giving evidence. The bruises on Eddie's legs turned out to be self-inflicted. He'd gripped himself so hard that he'd left marks. So who was to say it wasn't Lucy Taylor herself who'd stumbled hard into the furniture, pulled out her own hair in chunks and, in her seriously addled brain, decided for herself her son was better off kept hidden in the flat? Admittedly the rules have changed so, if a child's mistreated, anyone who's been present can be held responsible. But Harris had been smart, and Eddie Taylor came out of that flat well-enough fed, with nothing on his body that you could photograph to show a jury. And though the child was weirdly innocent of life outside, and sometimes very shy, he did appear surprisingly normal. Everyone said so. One keen, persuasive barrister for the defence, a nice new suit, and Harris could have been acquitted.

Nobody wanted that.

So they went at him sideways, since it was obvious the drug dealing and extortion, added to one or two counts of blackmail and intimidation that they rooted out, could clock up much the same sentence. In the end, on the principle of safety first, they went for that, just to be sure he'd be banged up.

And after that decision, once it was obvious that Eddie wouldn't have to tell his story in any trial, he came to me.

There he sat, in that chair over there, his thin legs dangling. He was a serious little fellow, still in the habit of peeking upwards surreptitiously, as though he'd kept that ratty fringe we'd seen in that, the first and only photo. (Judges move fast on a child's privacy.)

I wanted to start off with what he thought about the things that had happened since he left the flat. I can't remember quite how I began, but it was probably along the lines of, 'So, how's it going, Eddie?'

Just an open-ended question.

That didn't get us anywhere, but over the next few visits the child did seem to overcome his fear of saying anything at all in case it led to trouble. Gradually he became more and more confident about describing the small excitements of his new life with Linda and Alan. And that did offer some sort of a bridge for going back to talk of earlier days.

Then once, when I was asking him if he had visited his mother yet, he told me he was going there the very next day. With Rob.

'It's been a long time since you've seen her,' I ventured.

'When I was little,' he agreed.

That floored me. Obviously my first thought was that he'd conflated the mother who had been in hospital (and possibly, in his mind, cured) with the mum he had known so long ago, before Bryce Harris thrashed her into something else.

That didn't bode too well. 'Do you think she'll be pleased to see you?'

He nodded eagerly. I will admit, my stomach turned. We'd barely started, and that relentless *hope* young children specialize in had already sprung up, setting the poor lad up for horrid disappointment.

I said, 'She's been in hospital for quite a time.'

'She's in a nursing home now.'

'That's different, is it?' I asked warily.

'Linda says that it's better.' He studied his shoes for a while. 'We wrote a postcard. I chose it and it was an owl.'

'What did you say on the postcard?'

'I told her owls come out at night. And they eat mice.'

His voice brightened. 'Their eyes are fixed. That's why they have to turn their heads round if they want to see the sides.' He thought for a moment. 'They can't see things near to them very well, though. Only things far away. And they have special sorts of wings so they fly very quietly and don't frighten off what they were trying to catch. And some owls even eat fish. And baby owls don't all hatch on the same day.'

I couldn't help but smile. 'You managed to fit all that on a postcard?'

For just a moment, he looked puzzled. Then he admitted, 'No. Only the first bit.'

'But you know a lot about owls.'

'Yes. Mr Perkins took us to see a lady who kept lots of owls. She showed us a baby that was so tiny it weighed almost nothing.'

Even before the sessions began, Linda Radlett had filled me in on this Mr Perkins fellow. Indeed, she reckoned that the man had salvaged the child's life. 'If he's still on the planet,' she'd said to me, apparently quite sincerely, 'I'm going to track him down and write to tell him so.'

And it was clear that simply telling me about the owls made Eddie feel a little stronger. So we pressed on. They are short sessions and I wanted to prepare him for the visit to his mother because it was so obvious that any hopes he was harbouring were set to crash about his ears.

Poor little chap.

So we talked about how she might still be poorly. How it might be a much, much longer time before she would be even halfway better. (It was important not to let him go on believing that she would ever be the old Lucy Taylor again.) We talked about how it was Eddie's job to give her time, and keep his fingers crossed – yes, I said that. I know it isn't very professional. But he was only seven, for heaven's sake. And if the Social Services don't have the sense to tweak their guidelines about children having the right to see an 'innocent' parent more or less on demand, then what am I to do? How could I let him go in there thinking his mum was going to spin around, shout 'Eddie!' joyfully and squeeze him tight when I knew it was far more likely that she'd be slumped in a chair, clutching a handkerchief and staring blankly at the wall?

We talked about how, if he was upset after the visit, he could ask Linda for an extra cuddle. She would understand.

'She'll give me biscuits,' he said. 'And read the story without asking *me*.'

'Without asking you?'

'To do the easy words,' he explained. 'She'll read it all herself. Till I feel better.'

My watch was warning me that we were almost over time. I led him to the door. 'Bye, Eddie.' I squeezed his hand, but gently, since his finger ends still looked a little pink and raw. 'And good luck with the visit.'

'Fingers crossed,' he said.

Rob Reed, Social Worker

I put my hand up. It was a terrible mistake, taking Eddie to see his mum. The problem is, the things children imagine, left to themselves, are usually so much worse than simple fact. The times I've driven kids to prison to visit a mum or dad for the first time. All the way there, they're pale as grubs – can't answer the simplest question or focus on anything. Can't even taste the burger I buy them on the way.

Then in we go. All these new family suites have toys and jigsaws, book boxes, beanbags, even bright and cheerful mobiles dangling over the cots for the babies. It's like a daycare centre. The volunteers tend to be motherly ladies, pressing the young ones into accepting chocolate milk and fancy biscuits. No one is jangling keys or scowling. There are no bars in sight. And when the dad comes in, he and the warder who's accompanying him are as often as not sharing a joke.

The child I take home is a child I wouldn't recognize.

So when I heard he wanted to tell his mum how he could read a bit, and show her how well he could write his letters, I was very keen. Her bruises would have gone. The bald patches on her head would have grown out. (And, to be fair, most of them had.)

What I'd not bargained for was her dead face. It was a mask. I wondered if that monster Harris had somehow kicked her into some sort of embolism, or stroke. Lord knows, he'd bashed her hard enough to do permanent damage. She seemed dead from the neck up.

The woman who had led us to the room said, 'Here we are, Lucy. Here's your lovely little boy, come in to see you. Say hello to Eddie.'

She put her hand out – even touched his fingers – but her eyes stayed blank.

The minder prompted again. 'Come on now, Lucy. Say hello to Eddie. You've not seen him for a while, have you? But here he is, so let's try saying hello.'

She smiled then. Not a proper smile – the stupefied dead sort you might see on a widow's face as she thanked people after the funeral. She said, 'Hello.' The greeting was so flat you would have sworn she'd not met him before, and wasn't fond of children anyway.

I'd usually prompt a child to greet the parent back. 'Well, say hello, then.' I didn't, though. I don't know why. I think I might have been too angry to speak. I know the theory – misery breeds misery. And that is true, and we must understand and try to sympathize all the way up the family line, right back to where trouble began. But sometimes that is *hard*. Most of this misery is so *unnecessary*. If Lucy Taylor had only had the simple wits or guts to walk out on that man the very first time he gave her an aggressive nudge, none of this would have happened.

Sometimes I'd like to punch the parents of my clients really hard. Smash in their faces, in fact.

Oh, God! Don't write that down.

What happened after we left? Well, that was even worse. I got him in the car and waited while he strapped himself in. (He was still clumsy at that, he'd had so little practice on different cars.) We drove down the narrow nursing-home drive, and waited for the barrier to lift. Eddie said nothing, just stared out of the window for a while. And then he broke the silence. 'Rob, why did that woman call my mum "Lucy" all the time?'

My heart sank. I could feel it plummeting. I was too down at heart even to pick my way around what I guessed must be coming. Simply to get it over with, I asked the question outright. 'Because you thought her name was—?'

'Mum. And Harris always called her Bitch.'

Alan Radlett, Foster Parent

It worked out well, in a way. Because Rob took that painful little anecdote, along with one or two more, back to the panel, and they agreed that Eddie needed more time in a domestic setting, developing his social awareness and skills, before he could be thrown into the bear garden of primary school.

I didn't mind, and Linda was delighted. She had been making such good progress with his reading and arithmetic, explaining things, taking him places. She knew he would find school a massive strain, and every month we kept him home with us would pay off handsomely.

In any case, I liked his company. Usually I am quite glad, at half past eight each morning, to see the back of the kids we have and know that, unless they bunk off school and are delivered back to us, we're free till half past three. We're not spring chickens any more. I need the break. But Eddie was so easy to have around. (In that way, he was like Orlando.) He wasn't challenging. He didn't keep tiresomely pushing his luck, or testing the boundaries, like so many of them do. He was a bit like some well-meaning stray who'd had a rotten deal in life, knew it, and had the sense to recognize when he had landed on his feet.

Oh, he was strange. (I know, I know, they *all* are.) And yet the strangeness didn't seem to run right through his personality like letters stamped in red through seaside rock. It just burst out now and again. Sometimes it was almost amusing, like on that blazing hot day I sprawled on the sofa watching Wimbledon for hour after hour. On the last supermarket shop, we'd bought a case of ginger beer, and I must just have taken to the stuff because I sat there in that dripping heat, sipping all day.

(Amazing I didn't explode.)

Anyhow, Linda wandered in some time before supper. Hearing the 'phut!' as I prised up the tab of yet another can, she said to me, 'Blimey, Alan. How many's *that?*'

79

And then, from underneath my arm, we heard this clear little voice. 'Seven.'

'Never!' I told him. 'Never in your life.'

Linda went off to count up how many cans were left. 'He's right,' she reported back. 'You must already have finished seven.'

'You shouldn't have taught the little beggar how to count.'

'He could count anyway,' she reminded me. 'It was the taking away and stuff he'd never learned to do.'

I squeezed him. 'Is that right?'

'Yes,' he said proudly. 'I could count by myself even before I came.' And neither Linda nor I knew any way of telling him it was an odd habit for a little boy, to keep such close track of the number of times in a day he'd heard a man open a drink can.

Sometimes it wasn't funny at all. Take that time in the shed. He'd been in with me for an hour or so. 'Helping,' we called it. Our damn electric bill had shot up yet again, so I'd been fitting insulation sheets on all four sides, hoping to save myself from having to use the heater for so many months of the year. I'd fixed all the facing panels up again, and I was hammering back the nails on which I hung my tools.

Getting the last one in where I needed it was proving awkward. Maybe there was a wood knot in the upright behind. The first two nails bent and I threw them in the rubbish pot, and tried another. Same again. And then a fourth. I will admit that I was getting testy. I rather pride myself on how I work with tools, and Eddie was standing watching. So I reached out for three more nails, shoved two between my lips, and had another go at hammering one in.

To this day I'm not sure exactly what I said. Clearly I said it from between clenched lips. (Who wants to swallow a nail?) I think it was probably something as simple as, 'Now you're beginning to *annoy* me.'

I was talking to the *nail*!

But he had vanished from my side. Melted away. I didn't think much of it – simply tapped the nail's head into the wood slowly and carefully. And when I turned to see what he was up to, there he was, crouched in the corner. He had practically turned into a hedgehog ball, his head buried between his knees. You wouldn't think that even the smallest child could curl up so tightly.

'Eddie?'

I wasn't sure whether or not to touch him. Even a gentle hand can trigger such bad memories with some of these kids that they can go berserk. The place was full of dangerously sharp tools.

'Eddie?'

I would have gone to fetch Linda, except I was worried he would do a runner. And so I gradually talked him down. You know: 'Eddie, you're not back there. And I'm not Harris. No one in this house is angry with you. I was getting cross with the *nail*.' I just kept at it – very much like soothing a horse. (Not that I've ever done that.) And finally I must have got through to his frozen brain, because I sensed a relaxation in the tiny ball of him.

'Eddie, I'm going to touch you now. I'm going to put my hand on your shoulder and I want you to try to unfold. You don't have to look at me, but I do want you to stick out your legs and try to straighten your back.'

It took a bit of time, but finally he managed it. I led him in the house. He looked like death. Linda came back from next door, where she'd been fixing up to borrow wee Marie for the next swimming session. In front of Eddie I explained to her what had just happened. (He probably needed to hear a sensible account of it as much as she did.) She nodded and then led him off. I saw them sitting close together on the sofa. Her arm was round his shoulders. But it was only later, when she peeled off his shirt before his bath, that she saw all those splinters he had driven in his back when, trying to make himself invisible, he had slid down that rough, unsanded joist.

Linda Radlett, Foster Parent

After he wrote that postcard to his mother, one of the treasures I bought him was a tiny feathered owl. There was a shelf of them in Tanner's toy shop – spin-offs from something on telly. Each of them had a name on its pottery base. The one I chose was called Olly. (Oh, surprise me!) Eddie was thrilled with it. We had been having quite a time persuading him there was no need to hide the things he valued at the back of cupboards. So it was rotten luck that, just a few days later, Dolores came.

Dolores. I ask you. And anyone who looked less like a fancy Spanish dancer would be hard to find. The phone rang in the middle of the night. Less than ten minutes later she was on the doorstep, sturdy and scowling, with a nervous-looking female officer. Oh, she was angry. She had been lifted from her home at two in the morning, trying to intercede in a scrap between her mum and step-dad. It was the neighbours who had called the police as the fight ratcheted up. Both of the adults were, as the police officer put it, 'royally rat-arsed' and so Dolores had to be removed. (Guidelines.)

She was dead angry with the officer. And she was angry with us.

We had no choice but to stay up the rest of the night. I didn't fancy leaving Alan alone with her – she was the sort who'd make up stuff just to cause trouble. And he was worried about leaving me because Dolores looked as if she could pack a smart punch. She wouldn't go to bed. 'I'm not going to sleep in your stupid, smelly house! Forget it!' She turned a chair round and slumped down in it with her back to us.

So we made tea, and listened to her beefing about the fact that it was *her* business where she spent the night, not anything to do with us or the police. Then the tears started and we heard the sadder side of the story, about not being able to see her real dad any more because of his mean-minded girlfriend. And how her elder sister had given up on the whole family, and gone to ground in Sheffield. Poor Dolores was obviously so lonely, down-right rubbish at school and (as we gathered) pretty unpopular with teachers and classmates alike. She was a car crash of a child.

Alan kept listening while I fetched her a Coke. (She'd been quite rude about the idea of hot chocolate.) And when I took it to her, that's when I saw the tiny feathers around her feet. I'm sure she hadn't ruined the owl out of spite. Quite sure. She was just picking at it nervously, the same way Eddie gnawed his nails.

But Olly was now bald.

Someone came round to fetch her at eight the next morning, thank God, to take her home. She went off with a cheery wave (considering) and quite a pleasant, 'See you! Thanks for the Cokes and biscuits!'

I held the fort while Alan waited on the toy-shop step until they opened. Luckily 'Olly' was popular, so Alan bought two more, one and a spare, as if we were the parents of some toddler who always had to have two comfort blankets in case one of them got lost.

We had a chuckle later over our rusty acting skills. 'Eddie, you know you couldn't find your owl at breakfast? Well, here it is. I think that Alan must have moved it out of the way when he was clearing up.'

'Oh, sorry, Ed. It must have fallen down behind the television.'

I thought that we were home and dry. And I was sure I'd picked up every last one of the feathers Dolores shredded. But two or three of them had floated further than I thought, and Eddie had sharp eyes. It can't have been an hour before he noticed them, right up against the fender where the vacuum cleaner misses stuff.

He cradled the tiny feathers in his palm as he inspected the owl for bald patches. Then, 'Will I be going to see my mother again?' he asked.

'Any time you like,' I told him. 'All that you have to do is say.'

God, what a painful silence. It's ghastly trying to imagine what must run through these children's minds. I made some stupid excuse to leave the room in case he thought that I was waiting for him to agree and make a date. And though he followed me a minute later, he never said a word about his mother after that.

Charlotte Next Door

I was amazed to see him coming into our class. I hadn't realized he was nearly eight. Mrs Carlow brought him in. She had her hand on his shoulder and she was steering him, almost as if he was on wheels. She whispered something to Miss Bright, who turned to us and smiled and clapped her hands to stop us talking.

'Class, this is Eddie. He's new to our school, so I want everyone in this room to help him out until he finds his feet. If you see Eddie wandering down a corridor, you're to ask if he needs to know where he's supposed to go next. If you see him looking sad, I want to know about it. And if you have room for someone else to join in your game, I want you all to think of Eddie first.'

It's the same speech she made when Ethan came. And when Skye Lupin was moved down to our class after her stay in hospital because of that thing with her spine.

People were nice to him at first. But then I think that some of them began to think he was a little creepy. He sort of *copied* people. If we were playing shipwrecks in the gym, he'd pick on someone – usually Neil – and follow him round, a little too close behind. If Neil did a star jump, so would Eddie. If Neil scrambled up the bars, Eddie would wait till he'd come down again, then do exactly the same, and hurry to catch up. He did what he'd have done if he was teasing Neil. Except he wasn't. He was just *copying*.

He did the same to Astrid when we did painting in wet break. He copied everything she painted, in the exact same colours. Astrid went up to complain, and she and Miss Bright whispered together for a while. Only a little bit later, Miss Bright asked Eddie to help her carry some-thing along to the office. They were away for quite a while. I think I thought that she was probably telling him that he might have been allowed to copy people in that way back in his old school, but he couldn't in ours.

I didn't let on that he lived next door. Only to Emma. And I did tell her that she wasn't to *say* about him wearing Thomas the Tank Engine pyjamas or playing in the sandpit with a baby. I told her *twice*.

But she was cross because I'd given my last sweet to Surina, so she told on me. She slipped out of the lunch line and ran back to the classroom. I followed and I heard her telling Miss Bright, 'Charlotte is saying really mean things about the new boy.'

Miss Bright called me in too, and said she hoped I would try harder to be kind. I was so mad at Emma that I broke friends with her and went off with Surina. It was a horrid time till Emma and I made friends again. And after that I heard Surina crying in the lavatories, and I felt worse.

I don't think Eddie ever knew I'd told about the pyjamas. Or the sandpit.

Nothing was ever said.

Eddie

I'd never worn anything that bright and red before. The trousers were grey, but the school top was redder than ketchup. When I was taken in, on that first morning, everyone in my class just thought I'd moved there from some other school. Nobody asked about it.

The work was easy. By then I could read almost as well as everyone except for Priya. Miss Bright said my writing was neat. I had a bit of trouble with the number work because they were doing different things. But after Miss Bright called Linda in for a chat, and lent her the book, then Linda managed to explain that too, and it was easy as well.

Rob came to check on me, and I think that it was the uniform that made him push me a bit. 'I think your mum would like to see it. I think she'd be proud.' He tugged me back to face him when I moved away. 'You will feel better afterwards, I promise you. We'll go on Saturday. I'll fix it up.'

And it was all right, that visit. When we arrived, Mum wasn't in her room. The corridor was empty, so we just walked along, with Rob peering through the glass panels in the doors along one side, exactly like in school. He found her in a room with other people, sewing some brightly coloured ribbons onto a straw hat. Mum smiled as I came in, and when Rob steered me right in front of her, she said, 'Look at my bonnet!' and crammed it on her head, and laughed.

They'd cut her hair and it looked darker and redder. And she was in a flowery dress. The lady teacher said to her, 'Lucy, why don't you run along and take a bit of time with your little boy? The hat can wait.'

Mum made a sort of joke I didn't get. Something

about the hat having to wait till Easter. But Rob Reed chuckled, and explained to me on the ride home that it was an Easter bonnet, though I couldn't see why that made it a joke.

But it was really fancy, and my mum looked good in it.

She seemed a little baffled in the kitchen, so Rob made tea while we sat on two comfy chairs out in the lounge. She didn't ask me questions. She just smiled. I wasn't sure what I should do, so I just sat there. Then I said, 'I like your hair,' because I had heard Linda saying that to Marie's mother when we came back from the pool one day to find her hair was very different and really short.

Mum didn't answer, so I said, 'Did you cut it yourself?'

She frowned and shook her head as if there was a bit of water in her ears. And then she said, 'They did it.'

I told her, 'Linda takes me to the place on the corner. It's called La Mode.'

She didn't ask about Linda. She didn't seem to care. Then Rob brought in the tea. I saw him watching us as he went back to fetch the sugar and an extra mug to dump the tea bags in. I think he realized that I couldn't think of anything to say, so he told Mum, 'Look at what Eddie's wearing. It's his new school uniform.'

She fingered one of my sleeves. 'It's very red.'

'Isn't it?' Rob said. 'I think it suits him. Gives him a bit of colour.'

'One of the ribbons on my hat is red.'

'I thought your hat was lovely,' Rob said kindly and gently. 'After we've had our tea, you can go back and finish it if you like.'

She smiled so brightly that I realized that was all she wanted. So I drank my tea as fast as possible, though it was very hot. Rob stood up. So did I.

She stared at us as if she couldn't work out what was happening. Rob took her elbow and he sort of steered her back along the corridor into the room. They were all packing up their scissors and scraps and ribbons, but she didn't mind. She hurried in without even saying goodbye.

We went back to the car. As I was kicking at the gravel, Rob told me firmly, 'I think your mother looks miles better. She's put on weight, which makes her face look younger. That was a splendid Easter bonnet she was making. She still finds talking hard, but I think that she really liked your uniform. Don't you think she looks better and seems happier?'

I liked Rob, so I just said, 'Yes.'

Rob Reed

A lot of people just don't grasp some aspects of this job. Take Harry. He leaned over the allotment fence and said he thought that my first raspberries would probably be ready by midweek.

'Shame, that,' I said, 'because I'll be on Tyneside, so the birds will get them.'

'Tyneside?'

'Taking a boy in care to see his great-grandmother,' I explained.

'You get about,' he said. 'Were the two of them close?'

'As far as I know, they've never met – not since he was a baby, anyhow.'

Harry gave me quite a look. 'So what's the point in taking him all the way up there?'

'Family ties.'

He snorted. 'Your time. Your fuel. Though I suppose that it'll be Joe Taxpayer who picks up the tab. And all to no real purpose.'

How wrong can someone be? The drive was interesting. (I heard a lot about the way the Radletts run their life.) We stopped at Huddersfield, where Eddie tasted avocado pear for the first time – and mango, now I come to think. And when we finally reached the nursing home, the carer who showed us where to go told us that Mrs Lane had been 'bright as a button' until a few years before. 'It was her daughter going first that knocked the stuffing out of poor old Dinah. That's when she came to us.'

We walked along the carpeted hall, and there in a room with a bay window and a spare empty single bed was Eddie's great-grandmother – propped on a heap of pillows and snoring faintly.

The carer leaned over her. 'Dinah? Dinah? This is Eddie. He's your great-grandson. He is Lucy's boy.'

Mrs Lane opened her eyes and smiled seraphically.

'You know,' persisted the carer. 'Lucy. Your *grand-daughter*.'

Mrs Lane nodded hard, doing her best. 'Is it tea time?' she asked.

Eddie was mystified. The carer said, 'They love their piece of cake at tea time.'

A bell rang fiercely down the hall. The carer looked towards the door. 'Are you all right for a moment?'

'We won't stay long,' I said.

But she'd already gone. So I took up the reins. 'Mrs Lane, here is Eddie. He's come up to visit you and say hello.'

She was still smiling. 'Will *you* be having cake as well?'

'I hope so,' I said politely. And the whole benighted visit went on like that. But she was a member of Eddie's family and so a part of my job. Everyone needs a sense of self, and it is up to me to find a Life Story for even the children with the blankest slates. A newborn baby dumped on a street corner will leave the hospital with heaps of cheery photographs of nurses cuddling them, their very first blanket, even their 'favourite rattle'. No reason why we can't do better for someone Eddie's age. So I took one or two photos of his great-granny smiling benignly from her pillowed nest, with Eddie at her side.

The moment I let him, Eddie moved away and waited

by the window, peering watchfully at his great-grandmother. I hovered over Mrs Lane's bedside cabinet and the windowsill behind, looking for photos, small mementoes – anything that might give rise to questions that might lead to answers.

On the chest of drawers there was a photo of a woman with a child. I carried it across to Mrs Lane. She didn't need to look. She recognized the frame. 'That is my Clare,' she said. 'With little Lucy. Lucy hated socks. You'd get one on, but by the time you'd forced her tiny wriggling foot into the other, the first would be off.'

So. Eddie's mother, in his grandmother's arms.

I ploughed on for a while, trying to dig out more about this Clare. Friends? Workmates? Anyone who might have known something about her daughter Lucy's life before it was derailed by Harris. But it was obvious that Mrs Lane's brain ran only in small circles. I could have sat for weeks and heard about nothing but socks and cake.

I'd taken a couple of photos, anyhow. And Eddie had met a member of his family, even if he had taken to pretending he was invisible.

I waved the photo of Clare and Lucy at the carer when she came back. 'May I take a copy of this before we go?'

Watching her worrying about which tiresome issues of privacy something so simple might raise, I pushed a little. 'For *Eddie.*'

Her face cleared. Blandly she said, 'You know, I can't

see any reason why you and Eddie shouldn't slip out for a while to get some coffee.' She pointed to the bedside cabinet. 'And if you'd like to look at some other family photos while you're gone, peek in that drawer.'

Treasure trove! A score of photographs. And some kind soul who must have sat with Mrs Lane as she was gradually losing her mind had taken the trouble to inscribe the names of people in them on the back, along with the odd brief note. The careful italic handwriting offered its blessed cribs to future minders: *Harry – 'He was a devil when the drink was in.' Clare and best friend (Isabel? Elizabeth?) in Scarborough – 'Wind bitter. June. Chip supper after at Bertie's.'*

We took the lot. The nearest pharmacy had a copier. I needed to keep the names and notes attached to the right photo, so had to keep altering the controls to darken the lightly pencilled notes on the back enough to read, but keep the copies of the photographs from coming out too dark. I clipped the printed sheets in pairs while Eddie stood entranced by the sight of paper churning out of the machine.

One of the photos was in a transparent folder, and as I pulled it out a shower of photographs that had been tucked behind fell to the floor.

I picked them up. Crisper, more recent. Had they, perhaps, proved far too painful to be shared? Had they led only to tears? *'My Clare.' 'My Clare with Lucy.' 'Clare and Lucy at Saltburn.' 'Me and Clare.' 'Lucy and little Edward.'*

'Edward, aged 18 months.' 'Edward's second birthday.' 'Edward on the slide at Hurlabout playcentre.' 'Lucy and Edward.'

At last. At last! Something to shove in Eddie's Memory Box apart from that gloomy-looking, mouldering book!

Eleanor Holdenbach, Child Psychologist

Sometimes a child just walks away from disaster. People in my profession pass our lives with the unhappy and damaged. We spend a good few years reading about the myriad ways in which the psyche can be blighted. We study endless cases, discuss a thousand more, and meet the rest in person. Sometimes I think it stops occurring to us that it is possible to have an impaired childhood and a bruised soul, yet still come out of it close to unscathed.

But I have seen it often enough over the years. A drunken bullying father sends his car over a quayside and drowns. His daughter blossoms. The younger brother of a teenage drug addict accompanies his mother to the morgue where she identifies the messed-up, purple body. They walk away. Within a week the skin rash that's disfigured him for four long years has vanished, her blood pressure is back to normal, and you see the two of them smiling at one another in a supermarket aisle, discussing nothing more stressful than the coming meal.

And there was something of that sort in Eddie. He

wasn't interested in talking about Bryce Harris or his mother, or anything else in the past. He wanted to leave all that behind like some bad dream, and talk of his new school, his teacher (the aptly named Miss Bright, whom he adored), and after-school club on Tuesdays where, over the months I had my sessions with him, he seemed to learn to play everything from Snakes and Ladders to some sort of slimmed-down chess I never understood.

He sometimes talked about computer games (though it was obvious that Linda and Alan let him spend only enough time on those not to disgrace himself among his classmates). He told me what he was reading by himself, and what the Radletts read to him at bedtime. He talked about the films they let him watch. (A good bit of ground had to be made up there. I'd ask him, 'See anything good?' and he'd be telling me all about Dumbo the baby elephant, or Nemo the lost fish, as if he were the only person in the world who'd ever seen the film.)

So what we mostly did was talk about how he could best cope with others – especially those his own age. He'd certainly grasped the fact that he was different, and understood how it had come about. But he was keen to hide the fact as much as possible. So we explored how he might work on covering up the many gaps in his experience – how he might keep his friends, in short, from thinking him 'a weirdo' when he began to tell them things they'd known for years, or rushed into the classroom bragging about the fact that he had paddled in the sea. The *real* sea! Not even holding hands with Linda! Not even scared!

But he *was* teased in school, for all that Miss Bright was relentlessly stern with the rest of the class on poor Eddie's behalf. When he got low, I found our conversations drifted back, always, to Mr Perkins. He'd been a comfort to the child through those dark years, and it was to thoughts of the man that Eddie clearly turned in times of stress. I had persuaded PC Martin Tallentire to lend me a couple of the tapes still mouldering in police stores for want of anyone applying for their return. 'A therapeutic necessity,' I'd termed it in my request. And I admit that when I settled down to watch that sweet old fellow struggling in and out of his unstylish cardigan, and talking always as if the child watching was his *particular* favourite, I did feel my pulse settle and my spirits rise.

So there's still *goodness* in the world, I thought. Yes, there is goodness. One human being *can* help another through a vale of tears.

Rob Reed

If there is any way that Social Services can get the timing wrong, we'll manage it. We'd only had Eddie in the school for a few weeks when things began to move. Lucy's psychiatrist finally sent us his report (more than three months late), making it clear that he did not envisage it would be possible for her to care for Eddie, even in the longer term. It was the usual highly technical report about effects of trauma, neurological damage – pages of stuff. But the conclusion, written plainly at the end, was that Lucy's mental and emotional state would offer a seriously impoverished environment to any growing child.

And there was not much hope of things improving.

The panel met the following week and recommended, sensibly, that Eddie should be found a permanent placement.

Adoption, then.

I wasn't sorry. It was for the best. The ideal thing, of course, was for the Radletts just to keep him there. But they weren't licensed for anything more long term than emergency and transient placements. They were too old to permanently adopt a child of seven.

So we went looking.

II

Eddie

I don't remember all that much about the changeover. There didn't seem to me to be any specific day in which I was, as you might put it, 'handed over' to my new parents. I do remember the first time I met them. It was in Linda and Alan's living room. Nicholas and Natasha Stead were already sitting there when Alan and I came in after the walk back from school. He and Linda had warned me endlessly that they were coming. (Nobody sprang surprises on me at that time. If anything, coming events were usually described in such laborious detail that once or twice I even ended up with the idea that they'd already happened.)

There they sat on the sofa, side by side. Natasha had frizzy copper hair and wore a pretty dress. She sat back quietly. Nicholas (Natasha always called him Nicholas, never just Nick) seemed far more eager to get talking. He leaned forward so far I thought he might slip off the edge of the cushion seat and end up on the rug.

'Hi! So you're Eddie. Good to meet you. Linda was just this minute telling us . . .'

I wasn't listening. I was trying not to stare at his hand. It was a sort of fleshy stump. I'd not been warned about *that*. He clearly recognized I was distracted and, after a few more pleasant burblings, broke off to say, 'I see you're curious about my hand. It does look weird and horrid, doesn't it? It was an accident when I was young. But I'm quite used to it now. And no, it doesn't hurt. Not in the slightest.'

Do you know why I liked him from the start? Because he didn't begin this speech, which I imagine he had made a thousand times, with, 'I see you're staring at my hand.' It was that generous but honest choice of phrase, 'I see you're curious', that made me warm to him. (I *had* been staring, and I knew I had.) Before I had to think of a response, or even nod, he'd turned to Alan and started saying something about the number of butterflies drawn to the pinkish bush outside the window. I padded over to park myself on the floor between Linda's knees, the way I did sometimes when we watched television. She clamped me affectionately tight, and I can remember sitting there, listening to the four of them chatting about this and that, and, in the end, arranging to meet a day or so later at one of the pubs that had an outdoor garden somewhere between their town and ours.

I know that I'd been told exactly who they were. And yet I don't believe, that afternoon, I truly thought the Steads had much to do with me.

After they'd gone, Alan ruffled my hair. 'Come on, mate.'

I followed him down to the shed. He set me to my favourite job of sorting out his flowerpots. (I look back now and realize that he must have cluttered them deliberately over and over, so he would always have a reason to bring me down with him and keep me busy.) He hacked away at something growing in the way of the shed door. 'I'll tell you something about this climber, Eddie. It really knows how to annoy me.'

Finally he asked, 'So? What did you think of them?'

I don't know what I answered, though I've been told that later, maybe in bed that night, I'd asked if Nicholas was telling the truth when he said that his hand didn't hurt.

I don't remember that.

Or any trip to a pub garden. (Maybe it rained.) But gradually the visits to Nicholas and Natasha must have begun. I went first for an hour or two, along with Linda. Then on my own for one whole day. I got to know their rabbit, and later, when she came back from a day spent with a friend, I met their daughter. She was a couple of years older than me and, just like Linda and Alan's girl, she was called Alice. I do remember once or twice getting confused when people talked of either of the two. Sometimes I must have seemed quite thick.

And all the while, Rob Reed kept 'dropping in' and 'passing by', doing his job. His questions were different now. How did I feel about the Steads? Did I get on with Alice? Did I know she was adopted too? I did realize, didn't I, that I couldn't stay with Linda and Alan, but that the Steads would like to have me in their family. For good. Did I know what that meant? How did I think my mother (whom he had taken to calling Lucy all the time, even to me) would feel about that? Did I think she'd be glad that I was settled? Had I seen the new school?

It seemed to me that my new life was one long answering of questions. And, maybe because of Harris, I'd never learned the knack of looking honestly inside myself to find a real answer. All that I ever did was say what I thought would sound right. Often that was as easy as when Miss Bright asked, 'What's four times five?' and out came the answer, 'Twenty.' After all, if someone says, 'You can't stay where you are. So do you think you can be happy with these kind, smiling people offering you a home?' a child like me would never in a hundred years have realized that he could say 'No'.

Not that I thought that I would be unhappy. I didn't know how other people ticked, but I remember nothing, way back then, of tranquil, quiet feelings like simple happiness. I did feel triumph, yes. The very first time I managed to catch a really fat, wobbling rainbow bubble back on the plastic wand without popping it. Brilliant! Learning to work myself up on the park swings without a starter push, and sweeping my hair backwards along the ground in glorious celebration. And, joy of joys, finally getting the knack of balancing on a bike. I still recall the rush of pride. I couldn't sleep for longing for the morning, when I could pull the bike out of the shed again. Each skill tucked under my belt made me feel just a little more like everyone else, and moved me gradually further and further away from my old life in Harris's flat, making me safer and safer.

Yes, feeling safe was at the root of it.

That's why I'd fallen in love with Linda and Alan. I didn't care that they were old. I didn't care that everyone at school thought they were my nana and grandpa. I trusted them to protect me. I didn't even care that sometimes in the night the doorbell rang, and in the morning there would be a huddled, heavily breathing mound in the spare bed, or some pale girl with blurry blue tattoos screaming obscenities at Alan in the hall, or some other child my age mimicking me across the kitchen table as I ate, or snarling at Linda. These passing visitors could be as loud and nasty as they liked. There was a far, far deeper fear for me than their aggression – that, if I left Linda and Alan, things might work out so I ended up back with my mother.

It was the thought of that which made me sick with fright.

So happiness was nowhere in my mind, and I could easily agree with Rob that Nicholas was warm and loving, and Natasha endlessly smiling and kind. I suppose wheels turned. I know I had a special session with

Eleanor. And Rob explained the panel had decided that I could see my mother even after the papers were signed.

'Will I be sent to stay with her?'

I reckon Rob knew perfectly well what I was thinking. 'No,' he said. 'Never. Definitely not. You will be able to *visit* Lucy. But never on your own. And you can't stay the night.'

'Not ever?'

'No. Of course, so long as everything goes well, you can write letters and send cards and things. But as for seeing Lucy, the panel were quite clear. No sleepovers. Day visits only. And never on your own.'

And that, in my young book, was that. Done deal.

There were more overnight stays with Nicholas and Natasha. My bike and clothes seemed gradually to drift across to their house. It was agreed I'd stay for two last weeks with Linda and Alan because Miss Bright had picked me to be one of the singing oysters in the school play. But as soon as term came to an end, Linda and Alan went off on holiday while Rob drove me to Fairhurst for my first long, uninterrupted visit.

'See how things go,' said Rob. 'See how you settle down.'

I *loved* my room. They had transformed it since my last short stay and I couldn't believe how bright and glossy it looked. I was allowed to choose my own duvet cover. I could tell that neither Natasha nor Nicholas was crazy about the one I picked, but they had promised me.

Natasha hid her panic well, and Nicholas's remark – 'Brave fashion choice!' – held only a hint of sarcasm.

Only Alice was rude. 'Ee-*ew*! That's awful, that is!'

Next morning, we went shopping again. Nicholas led me along the strangely crooked-looking streets of their small town and bought a whole new school uniform for me in a grown-up-looking grey. That's when it finally dawned on me that I was truly starting over. There would be visits back to Linda and Alan, yes. I had been promised that. But I'd been moved.

I know I cried my eyes out secretly in bed that night, thinking that I would never see Miss Bright again.

Alice

I was excited. Alison, my best friend, had four cheery brothers and I was jealous. (Back when I lived with Mum, I had had an imaginary cousin. His name was Robert, but he was tied up in my mind with the old floaty curtains that I used to watch while I was going to sleep; and though the boxes of my own stuff went with me to Natasha and Nicholas's house over the months that Mum was ill, Robert got left behind.)

Natasha let me in on all the getting ready for Eddie. I helped her choose the shade of yellow from the paint samples she splashed across his bedroom wall. I went with them to fetch the shiny new table and the matching chair. Natasha chose the curtains, but let me pick the one I liked best out of the three rugs in the soft-furnishing department that she said 'sat with them nicely'. (That's why she was so horrified when Eddie chose that purple duvet cover with the dinosaurs – though Nicholas told her firmly, 'No, it's Edward's choice.')

The thrill wore off. In fact, I look back now and wonder if it wasn't more the shopping that excited me, rather than Eddie. He was so *quiet*. Not a bit like Ali's brothers. He didn't even move around the house much. He sort of stayed wherever he'd been left. He never argued. Nicholas would watch me mooching about, not really doing anything, just getting more and more bored, and he'd get irritated. 'For heaven's sake, Alice, why don't you go out in the garden?'

I'd give him the evil eye and tell him sullenly, 'I've already *been* in the garden.' But Eddie would go out as if it were an order, even if till that moment he'd been perfectly content doing one of his jigsaws.

He adored jigsaws. Natasha asked him once, 'What is it about them that gets you, Edward? Is it the the pictures, or getting finally to put the last piece in, or what?'

Do you know what he said? He said, 'I like to think of all those tiny little bits going into the exact right place, all comfy and cosy and safe.'

He said it. But he didn't bother to look up. So it was only me who saw Natasha and Nicholas eyeing one another over his head.

It was a weird look they exchanged.

I just thought he was rather odd.

Edward

I became Edward. Natasha and Nicholas didn't exactly come out and tell me openly, 'We prefer Edward.' But that's what they called me, and when I went to my new school, that is the name the teachers used. I must have seemed a little dense, taking so long to respond till I got used to it. Before, when I'd been Edward, it had been Alan ticking me off for leaving stuff about. 'Edward James Taylor, is this *your* clutter left all over the floor? How about coming back to clear it up?'

It was what Linda, with a smile, referred to as my 'Sunday name'. But from the start Nicholas and Natasha had used it almost as often as they called me Eddie, and once I'd moved into their house they used it more and more. The notes the teachers gave me to bring home always had 'Edward Stead' written along the top because I'd been advised by Rob to use that name at school. 'It's simpler. But you'll keep the name Taylor for quite a time, in case you change your mind.'

He meant about being adopted, although he didn't spell that out. He'd already brought round what he called my Life Story Box. I'd never seen it before. It was a sturdy yellow cardboard carton with flaps tucked in on top.

He dumped it on my bed. 'Here you are. Everything except the stuff Natasha and Nicholas will have to keep safe for you.'

'Stuff like my birth certificate?' (I was determined to keep track of the replacement. Rob had seemed disappointed that there was nothing written in the space for Father's Name. But I was simply thrilled to know my proper birthday at last. And Priya had assured me in front of everyone in my old class that I was a Leo. Loyal and strong, she said, just like a lion. And someone who liked changes.)

'Yes, they'll keep the stuff like that. But all the rest of your things are in this box, and you get to look after them.'

Prising up one of the carton's flaps, I spotted my school report card from the term before, and one of the *Frog and Toad* books.

'Want to go through it?' suggested Rob. 'Maybe show some of the things to Natasha and Nicholas?'

I shook my head and slid the box away, under my bed. Later, in private, I pulled it out and rooted through. Olly the owl, of course. (I took him out and put him on the shelf above my bed.) All of the little things that I'd been given to encourage me when I was learning to read. One or two muddy paintings from back when I was still getting the hang of rinsing my brush between colours. The photo Alan framed of me dressed as an oyster, standing between Priya and Jamie. Two cards from my mother's nursing home, probably written by someone else but both signed 'Mum'. The photocopies I had watched come churning out of the machine that day with Rob in Gateshead. Some grubby birthday card a policeman found in our flat. The musty book that Rob took with us when he first led me away.

And underneath, in piles of four that neatly lined the bottom of the box to make it look far fuller than it was, all of the ancient video tapes of Mr Perkins.

But all of it was stuff I'd left behind. I was a Leo now. Priya had told me that Leos liked changes and my whole life had changed. And so I shoved the yellow cardboard carton back, out of sight and mind, under the bed.

There was no one like Miss Bright at my new school. No one to lead a crying child into the cushion corner to hear about the kitten who had been run over, the brand-new model glider whose wings had been snapped off by some rough baby sister, or details of classroom spite. No one to tell us sternly, 'It's only *bullies* who call it "telling tales". Everyone else knows that it's letting grown-ups know why someone in the class is feeling unhappy.'

You had to stand up for yourself at Tandy Lane Junior School. Nobody picked on me, but still I found each day exhausting. I didn't know that at the time, of course. I just came home and shoved Nicholas's great black leather-lined earphones on my head and listened to his favourite Roxy Music tracks till he loomed over me, pointing to the time. 'OK, poppet. Feeling better? Ready to face the world as well as the music?'

He was an architect who worked from home. Inside his office was a massive sloping board on which he pinned his drawings and plans. I used to stand behind and marvel at how he used his elbow rather than his ruined hand to hold down rulers or papers. Appointments and site visits must have been arranged so he could meet me every weekday for a while at the school gates. I didn't realize quite how many outside appointments he must have till I got tonsillitis. In between barking coughs, I heard him on the phone over and over.

'I can't apologize enough. I realize you're probably already on the way . . .'

'I'm sorry but we must postpone the site meeting at noon.'

'This chat about the plans. You couldn't possibly reschedule it for later in the day? Or meet me here? You see, we have a sick child in the house, and my wife can't get back till after five.'

And that was early for her. Natasha ran a rental agency. I never understood the business properly. It seemed to cover, not just flats and cars, but huge marquees and smart green and gold vans with things like mobile bars and giant cooking cauldrons that could be wheeled down ramps and set up anywhere for outdoor events. Sometimes, at weekends, Natasha would be gone even before I woke, and not come back till after I was asleep.

(Next morning she'd be in the foulest mood about her job. Alice and I would hear her crabbing through their half-open bedroom door. 'Christ, Nicholas, you wouldn't *believe* that family! Rude, arsy lot!' We'd hear her wrenching open a dresser drawer. 'Do you know, at one point the bride's father even pulled out his copy of the contract and starting stabbing his stinking, cigarette-stained fingertips at one of the clauses! I could have bloody clocked him!' The drawer slammed shut. 'I tell you, Nicholas, that Beck family is going right at the top of our "Sorry, we're fully booked" list!')

She took me to see a marquee. ('You've never seen one? Oh, Edward. You *must* have. Surely you've been inside a circus tent!') She knew my history. Rob had assured me that he'd told them everything. But still the idea that there were a host of things I'd simply missed kept slipping out of her brain.

I quite liked that. If I was not the first thing on her mind, maybe that was because I didn't need to be.

Maybe I was all right.

Certainly Alice seemed to think so. She welcomed me with great enthusiasm, showering me with small gifts. And even after that wore off, as it soon did, I never got the feeling Alice thought that I was odd. I can remember thinking that we were the same in some ways. Secretly I felt pleased when I heard Alice never knew her own real dad. And when she was my age, her mother had got sick.

Then sicker. Alice did have an uncle, but he'd done little more than send the occasional present and Alice's mother clearly hadn't thought he was the right person to take care of Alice. So in the end she'd got in touch with Social Services. I didn't ask too many questions, but I could tell from how Natasha and Nicholas talked that they had got to know Alice's mother well while they were caring for her daughter during the last few months.

But I was still surprised when, one wet afternoon, Natasha poked her head round my bedroom door while I was cutting out another line of grey scales for the dinosaur I had to make for school. 'Edward, can I ask you a giant favour?'

I looked up.

'Would you mind coming with Alice and me in the car? Nicholas can't keep an eye on you in the house because he has to rush across town to see a client, and it's Alice's mother's birthday.'

She saw my look of utter bafflement and made a face. 'God! Sorry, Edward. I should explain. Today is one of the days that we put flowers on Tamara's grave.'

I must have still looked confused.

'I know,' she said. 'But, you see, Alice loved her very much. So it's a nice way of remembering. We do it twice a year – on Alice's own birthday, and on her mum's.' Natasha waved a hand across her face. 'You won't need to come close if you don't want. I can park on the drive and you can stay in the car. We're never there too long.'

And so we went. As usual, Alice raced ahead to bag the car's front seat. 'Careful!' Natasha warned. 'It's flowers you've got there, not an entrenching tool. Don't bash them all about.'

Alice just stuffed the bright bunch in my hand. 'You take them. More room in the back.'

I knew that a real brother would have said, 'No. They're *your* flowers. *You* sit here.' But I'd already learned to do what Alice said. In any case, the flowers weren't for her. They were for someone dead.

You wouldn't have thought so. All the way across town, Alice was prattling cheerfully about some spend-thrift friend of hers who was called Mary. 'So it turns out she's bought *another* locket, and there was nothing wrong with the one she had except that it kept falling open, and that could have been fixed, and Sarah says . . .' On she went, on and on, while I amused myself by clouding the rain-stippled window with my breath and drawing faces till Natasha swung the car between two massive gate posts.

Slowly she drove around the gracious curves between the lines of gravestones. Then she stopped.

Alice twisted her head to order me out of the car. 'Come on, then.'

Natasha tried to rescue me. 'I thought that Edward might prefer to—'

But Alice wasn't listening. 'Be careful with the flowers!' She'd already left the car, slamming her door shut behind her. Slavish as ever, I followed her across the soggy grass to the grave. Once there, as if obeying some invisible order, Alice burst into tears. Natasha slid an arm round her shoulders and the rain poured down. All about was gloomy green dark. I'd only brought my thin school waterproof and I was cold, standing there waiting for Alice to finish dabbing and sniffling. The bunch of flowers was getting heavier by the minute. I hadn't realized it was gathering rainwater until a sudden creak of cellophane released a stream of it onto my foot.

Too late, I jumped to the side. Seeing me, Alice sighed. 'Here. Hand them over. Honestly, I'm all right now.'

Natasha steered me away, but when I turned to look, though Alice had her back to us, I knew that she was talking to her mum, under the ground.

Natasha ushered me into the front seat beside her. 'I know you're frozen. But I don't want to start the car in case Alice thinks we're rushing her.'

Another small thing learned. To use the heater in a car, you have to start the engine.

'That's OK.'

Natasha patted my knee. 'You're a good boy.'

I waited, trying not to shiver, till Alice came back. She must have been halfway across the grass before she realized she still had the flowers. Back she rushed, to dump them against the headstone before running back to wrench the car door open on my side.

'How come Edward's in the front?'

Natasha, who had only that moment turned on the engine, said, 'Just to be near the heater.'

I took the hint. Alice stepped back to let me out. It took an age to warm up on the long drive home.

The dead seemed to be closer than the living. Natasha never once mentioned my mother. But every now and again, Nicholas would steer me quietly into his office where, even if he left the door ajar, we'd not be overheard. 'What about you, pal? Feel like visiting your mum?'

I'd shake my head.

'But you will tell us when you change your mind?'

I nodded, determined to pretend I hadn't noticed he had recently changed from saying 'if' to the more threatening 'when'.

He'd ruffle my hair. 'Your call. I was just checking.'

He'd let me scramble past and up the stairs. So I was happy enough living at Fairhurst. Rob's visits became shorter, almost peremptory, as if he had more pressing things to do than check on me. Linda and Alan gradually backed off, with postcards and small gifts taking the place of visits. The weeks and months went past. I grew out of my clothes, and in and out of others. I learned to rollerblade, to kick a ball into goal, play 'Planet Attack!' as fast as anyone in my class, and even dive off the springboard at the local pool. I learned the layout of the streets around the house, and which of the dogs and cats I saw

117

about the place belonged to which of the neighbours.

Fairhurst had gradually become my home.

George Atkins, Class Teacher, Tandy Lane Junior School

I wouldn't say that he was anything special. Bright, obviously. And he did the work. But if you'd asked me, after he'd been gone from us for a few years, I'd never have been able to put a face to the name.

Except for that one day. I'd had a sleepless night and wasn't in the best of moods. I set them all to do a piece of written work. Usually I give them choices, but on this one occasion I just scrawled on the board the first thing that sprang to mind.

Ladybird.

Normally, I would have noticed the hush that fell across the room. I expect I thought the kids had picked up on my ratty mood and had the sense to keep their heads down.

But it wasn't that, of course. Tara crept to my side and whispered, 'Mr Atkins. Edward is crying.'

I looked up from the marking I'd been ploughing through and I felt *terrible*. The boy's face was a sheen of tears. In all my years of teaching, I've never seen a child look so distraught. Practically *haunted*.

I almost had to lift him from the chair. He couldn't

118

walk. His legs gave way under him. There are strict rules about the way we interact with pupils. I never gave them a thought. I simply picked him up and carried him along to the office. Somebody phoned the Steads, who came to fetch him.

That night his parents rang, each listening on a separate extension, to ask what set him off.

'They were just writing about ladybirds,' I said. 'Apparently, he copied down the title and that was that.'

The boy was back in school next day, a little pale but generally OK. We knew he'd had a difficult past, so I did not ask questions – well, not of Edward. But a year or so later, shortly before he left us, I saw his mother in the entrance hall and dared to ask, 'Did Edward ever tell you what set him off that day?'

She shook her head.

That is the only reason I remember him.

Edward

Bit by bit, over the years, I must have got the knack of acting normally. But even after moving up to secondary school I worried constantly about what others made of me: how they might wonder about the way I knew some things, but not others; what they might think about the way I ate or spoke, or asked or answered questions. I think I worried that, without even realizing, I might let drop a trail of clues to lead them into guessing things about my mum and Harris. The idea terrified me. I'd hear their whispered comments about Nicholas's ruined hand and couldn't bear the thought that anyone might link me to worse: that hooded man who'd shoved against his escorts so aggressively as he was dragged into court; a photo in a hospital file of the bruised woman with the bleeding scalp who was led out that day.

So I came home dead tired every afternoon. After a while, Nicholas would gently but firmly prise off the earphones that blocked everything except the softly swirling beat that helped to banish all the day's frustrations and anxieties. I'd follow him into the kitchen, where he'd make tea, and I'd drink juice and root through the biscuit barrel while the questioning began.

'Good day?'

'All right, I suppose.'

'And Mrs Hunter?'

'She was OK.'

'How was your music lesson?'

'Not bad.'

'Got any homework?'

'Just a bit.'

This last was my daily lie. I did my homework in the old lavatory along the furthest corridor. Nobody used it. There was no sign on the door and I only knew a lavatory was in there because I'd been sent along to the janitor one morning to tell him one of the juniors had been sick. That's where he stored his bucket. The smell of disinfectant wasn't going to bother someone like me, and so in the long lunch breaks I'd got in the routine of hanging around the others for a while, then slipping away. I had no special friend to notice I'd picked up my school bag from the pile against the wall, and casually ambled off. I'd stroll along the corridor as if I might be making for the water fountain at the end. And when the coast was clear, I'd slip inside the tiny room and bolt the door.

The lavatory had a lid so I could sit quite comfortably in cool, tiled silence, finishing every scrap of work I had to do so that the moment Alice slammed her way into the house, bursting with news about her own day in school, I would be free to slip off yet again, upstairs this time, to do what I loved most.

Read.

I'd grown a passion for books. It seemed to me that every single one I read offered me hints on how to be more normal. I felt as if they had been written just for me, to give me private, safe and restful lessons in how other people lived. More, they created in me gathering confidence that there were endless ways to go about the business without rousing suspicion. The family in one book might be chaotic, with every getting-up time a riot of alarm clocks and nagging, and every meal a horde of people shouting about what they did or didn't want to eat; an endless run of noisy arguments and jokes, laughter and tantrums and tears. But in the next book I picked up, the parents and the children might bow their heads in prayer around the table before they quietly and politely passed the plates.

They were all *families*.

And you could learn about so many things. Wet camping trips in leaking tents, and luxury holidays in sun-kissed hotels abroad. Journeys up steaming rivers or over treacherous glaciers. Children who ran around in scruffy tops and muddy jeans, and children whose mothers dragged them into designer shops to spend a fortune on a blouse that would be far too small within a week. Sometimes, when I was in the middle of a book, I'd catch a wisp of memory, and be reminded of a visit we had made with Mr Perkins. But those had mostly been to adults doing interesting things. Now I was able to peek into the daily lives of people my own age.

They were all different. All of them fascinated me. And the joy was that I could see into their lives with no sense that I was a trespasser – doing what people in my junior school used to call 'goggling' as they put their arms around their work to keep it from prying eyes, or moved behind a shield of coats to finish a whispered conversation.

Books were so *different*. You could read about people of all sorts, all ages: brave, clever, miserable, amusing, shy. People from foreign countries. People who'd lost a leg in battle, or starred in films. You found out what they thought, saw how they ticked, learned everything about them, down to the thoughts that haunted them in their beds. Your worries might be about other things, but from the books you read at least you'd learn you weren't alone in worrying. You need no longer fear that there was something odd in that.

Nicholas thought I was a laugh, with all my weird observations and handy hints culled from the reading matter I brought home from the libraries at school and in town. I'd wander into the kitchen to find him scowling at an almost-empty bottle of wine. 'Just freeze it,' I'd advise.

'*Freeze* it?'

'The mother in *Harriet's Happy Café* always froze left-over wine so she could put it into casseroles later.'

'Really?'

'Yes. And she kept a bag of grated ginger in the freezer for when they next had a stir fry.'

'Now that is *brilliant!*'

He was so easy to amuse and please. I'd ask him, 'Did you know that the Duke of Orleans shot larks with the corks from his champagne bottles?' Nicholas would roar with laughter. 'No. I did not know that!' Natasha, I see now, was more inclined to keep her distance. Of course she was busier, and didn't work from home. Still, when she came back at night I always felt that she was happier if – how can I put this fairly? – if Alice and I had been somewhat tidied away. If we'd been fed already, she was pleased, and if the general round-up of evening household tasks had been completed before she came through the door, she was delighted – not at all like Nicholas, who showed his disappointment if he came home from a late meeting to find that we'd already gone our separate ways: Alice to the computer she still nagged to be allowed to take back to her bedroom where she'd apparently 'abused the privilege' by using it too late at night.

And me to my books.

That's how I ended up back in the box under the bed, so many years after I pushed it there. Blame my school. Alice, by then, had been moved to some expensive girls' academy in the hopes of keeping her in control. (Yes, I still listened at doors.) But my school was an easy-going place. Natasha showed her irritation every term when she saw my report cards. 'What *is* this? What am I supposed to make of all these stupid shaded boxes? Why can't the teachers send home a simple bloody sentence to tell me how you're doing? Can't they *write*?' There was a deal of quiet talk about the possibility of moving me somewhere else. Then counter-whispers about how 'yet more upheaval' might be bad for me. I even overheard Nicholas suggest that they phoned Rob for advice. (Natasha wasn't keen on that, insisting that anyone in Rob's profession was likely to disapprove of private schools purely on principle.)

So nothing happened. I was allowed to drift along, and not unhappily.

Until the school library closed for nine weeks for the repair of the roof.

I managed for a while, with Nicholas driving me to the library in town every now and again. (Alice had given up on reading and taken to boys instead.) But then one of his architectural projects went awry, and he was working all hours to stay on top of things.

So there I was, early one weekend morning. No homework. Nothing to do. And nothing in the house I hadn't read before or didn't want to read at all.

Natasha pounced. 'Stop *moping*, Edward! You're driving me insane. You have been wandering around for two whole hours. Can't you do something useful? Bake a cake, cook supper or something?'

'Not in the mood.'

'How about mopping the conservatory? The floor's a mess.'

'No thanks.'

'Well, what about your bedroom? That's a real tip. Why don't you go under that bed of yours and sort out all your grown-out-of toys and games, so I can take them to the charity shop.'

'I promise you I'll do it soon.'

But I had pushed my luck, prowling so irritatingly around the house. 'No, Edward. You can do it now. It's that or mopping the floor.'

So up I went, and tugged the whole mess out from where it had been shoved, behind the bed cover. Old toys and jigsaws. Plastic figures from crazes at school. Board games with missing pieces. Mud-encrusted football boots that can't have fitted for years. A heap of comics, magazines and Alice's tennis racquet, reluctantly lent to me and mislaid for so long they'd had to buy another.

And, right behind all that, my old Life Story Box.

At first I didn't suppose I'd even look inside. I simply hauled it out to clear space under the bed before I made decisions about what to shove back. I started with Alice's racquet, for fear of sparking everyone off again about the fact that I'd lost it in the first place. Then I began to put things into 'Trash' or 'Treasure' piles, just as Natasha did when she was clearing the conservatory or other rooms of all the stuff Alice and I left about. Naturally, when I got down to all the awkward things I couldn't decide whether to chuck or save, I lost the will to carry on. Pushing aside that messy heap, I opened the box.

Rescue! Escape from drudgery! A book!

I had forgotten it was there because it had been in the box since almost before I could read. It had meant nothing to me. It did now! Who would have thought the *stink* of it could last so many years? I was *thirteen*. Yet, in an instant, I was back inside that flat, astonished to be able to turn the book the right way up with fingers whose ends weren't bleeding raw, or stare at the silvery italic title without first tossing back my matted hair.

The Devil Ruled the Roost.

What had Rob muttered as he led me out? 'Didn't he just!' And now, repeating the words under my breath exactly the way Rob had, it came to me for the first time that he'd had Harris in mind.

So how long had it been?

Six years! Bryce Harris might be out of prison now. If we met in the street, I'd know that it was him, but he would pass me by without a second glance – me in my smart school trousers and my fresh white shirt, with hair that had turned lighter in the sun as the years passed.

He wouldn't recognize my voice, of course, because he'd barely heard it.

I was safe from him.

Oh, but the smell of that book! It wasn't just a sour, musty, clinging stench. It was a living memory of cold unhappiness, a grim reminder of all those endless hours of terrified waiting and gathering dread. The room blanched white. I tried to do what Linda taught me all those years ago – lower my head between my knees, breathe out as slowly as I could, and count to ten. Her comforting soft strictures now echoed through my mind. 'Steady, my poppet! Steady! You're safe now. He'll never get to you again. Now, come on, Eddie. Get control. Breathe out. That's right. Keep breathing. Slowly, slowly. There's my own precious baby. There's my boy . . .'

Gradually the panic passed. I wiped the sweat off my face and picked up the book again. This time I opened it and read the first line. '*Right from the very start, my life was strange.*'

Hooked.

Scrambling to my feet, I went into Alice's bedroom. On the shelf over her bed there sat a little spinney of tubes and bottles and sprays. I sniffed at them all. Some were so sickly I couldn't think how she could put them anywhere near her hair or face or body. Some smelled quite nice, but didn't seem quite strong enough for the job.

So in the end I settled on *Teen Flower*, which claimed to be '*eau-de-cologne* for the fresh girl about town'. I chose it partly because I liked the smell of it and partly because the bottle's fussy, flowery design meant Alice wouldn't be able to tell how much of the stuff had gone. Smuggling it into the garden, I sprayed the cover of the book all over. Then I replaced the bottle exactly where it had stood before, and went back to my room to read.

You'd think that story had been written for me.

It was the strangest tale. Just like myself, this boy had spent his early life hidden away. His mother had been clever, persuading him that he was ill. She kept him in a small back room, away from any windows through which he might be seen.

Like me, he had been rescued. Just the same way, in fact, after a neighbour caught a glimpse of him one day and started wondering. Like me he'd gone to a kind family where he'd felt safe and happy. Then they had moved him – found some peculiar uncle miles away and sent him off. That's when the worst trouble began. I *loved* the book. The plot was stuffed with ancient secrets and lies. There was a constant threatening mood about the story. And all the time, the boy was wondering about those early years. About his mother. What had she been about, locking him up like that? How could she possibly have thought it was the best thing to do?

And that's what set me off. Oh, I read to the end. (I couldn't stop. I had to know what happened.) But even as I flicked the pages past, I was distracted. And once I'd clapped the book shut at the end, the thoughts swept in. What was my mother *doing*, letting herself turn into Harris's punchbag, derailing her life and mine? By the time we were rescued, even I recognized she had less chance than I did of doing something – anything – to save us. She had become a mess, incapable of making a simple plan to listen to Harris's footsteps echo away down the stairs, unlock the door and take my hand to lead me down the stairs and out, into the sunlight.

No one becomes a shivering bag of terror overnight.

How did it happen? How could her need to stay with Harris have been more important than keeping me happy and safe? How stupid can you be when someone slams a fist into a cupboard door, or in your face, then says, 'See what you made me do? That's *your* fault, that is!' Nobody with a forkful of brain has to believe the damage and the violence is their fault, and feel obliged to stay around to try to sort it out or make amends – try to do better in future – creep around like a mouse, pathetically desperate not to set off the furies.

Great thugs like Harris don't rule the entire *world*. There are police stations. There are refuges. There are people like Rob Reed.

There was the door! Why didn't we walk through it before he started locking it on the other side whenever he went out?

Why didn't we walk through it before he punched her *stupid*?

And once the book had set me thinking, I couldn't stop. I couldn't *understand*. All of those times I'd sat in Eleanor Holdenbach's room, watching the clock hand creep round as she'd run through her questions! Was this what she'd been trying to get a handle on in all those sessions? I hadn't let her in. I'd acted stupid. No. Not *acted* stupid. I had *been* that way, not even understanding that there were feelings that I might have had and should have had. Feelings like disappointment, curiosity, mystification. Stronger than that! How about a sense of pure betrayal at realizing that I must, for my mother, have counted only as second best.

All just a shadow of the feelings I was having now. Like surging *rage*. What sort of mother doesn't try to protect her son from someone like Bryce Harris?

Or was she as stupid as me? Had she been reckoning

that, just so long as his filthy fists and boots were landing only on her own soft flesh, and not on mine, that was protection enough?

Alice

I saw him in the mirror once. Just his reflection. I was walking past the living room to get my trainers out of the conservatory. I must have been in socks. He didn't hear me, anyway. And he was standing staring at himself in the tall mirror.

Just standing there, in his school uniform, gazing into his own eyes. I don't know why I stopped to watch. Maybe because he spent so much time surreptitiously watching me, I thought it was fair play.

Then suddenly he raised a hand to push his fringe back off his face. And then he smiled. It wasn't a real smile. He was just seeing what his face looked like, the same way Jessica and I do when we are working out what comes out best in photos.

He watched himself for a while, then let the smile drop.

Just like that.

I would have teased him, but he looked so horribly alone and sad. I just rushed past to find my shoes and get upstairs again, out of the way.

Eddie

My big mistake was letting Nicholas and Natasha sense that my attitude towards my mum had hardened horribly. They wouldn't let me just be done with my old life. Nicholas said to me gently enough one day, 'Edward, you don't think this would be a good weekend to see your mother?' (No doubt at Rob's suggestion, he'd tried to switch to calling her Lucy all the time, but kept on slipping back into old habits.)

I made a stab at pretending that I hadn't heard. But he persisted. 'It's been three months now. And that's too long – both for her and for you.'

'Not for me,' I said sourly.

He put his arm round my shoulder. 'You can't pretend she isn't *there*. Or that she's not your mum. Or that she isn't how she is.' He gave me a little shake. 'I know the visits can be pretty grim for you. And probably they do seem pointless, what with her being so away with the fairies. But seeing her does *matter*, so we ought to go.'

I shook him off. 'If you think it matters that much, then *you* go!'

Now that was not like me. A look of deep concern came over his face, and then he called my bluff. 'All right, I will. I'll go this afternoon. I won't stay more than half an hour because I need to get the car into the garage for tomorrow's servicing. But I will go. And I'll be leaving here straight after lunch.'

So after lunch I hurled myself into the car at the last minute, as he was backing down the drive. I wouldn't speak to him for the first half of the journey, and I was sullen for the rest. He must have been exasperated by the time we reached the home. But I went through with it – went through the swing doors, spoke as civilly as I could to Harry on reception, pretended to smile at my mother, admired the set of rag dolls she had made, said that I liked the new curtains in her room. I offered her one of the cakes that Nicholas had brought along with us, and nodded obediently as Nicholas listed whichever school and sporting achievements of mine he could dredge up from the last weeks.

And it was over. We were in the car and starting on the journey home. 'There!' he said, maybe a shade too smugly. 'That wasn't so bad, was it.'

I lost my temper. 'Yes, it was!' I shouted at him. 'I hate it! It's *pointless*! Her brain's so scrambled that she doesn't even really know who I *am*. She certainly doesn't *care*. She is more interested in her stupid rag dolls than anything at all to do with me. I don't know why we have to bother to come!'

He'd had enough as well. 'Well, we just do! Until you're old enough to make your own decisions.'

Here was a big surprise. 'How long will *that* be?'

'I don't know!' I realized how upset Nicholas was when he swung the car out into the busy line of traffic in far too narrow a gap. 'Ask Rob. When you're fourteen?

Sixteen? How should *I* know how long adoption orders keep us to the rules?'

I stared. 'We only keep on coming here because of some stupid *rule*?'

'What did you *think*?' he snapped. 'That Natasha and I believe it's a grand idea to drag you back here four times a year to be reminded of something that should never, ever have happened to you in the first place?'

'Oh.'

I sank back in the seat. I hadn't realized.

The ride back was as quiet as the journey there had been. But there was quite a different atmosphere inside the car. Companionable exhaustion. I think that I felt older, realizing what was going on and knowing one day, not so far away, I'd have a choice.

So after that I wasn't quite so difficult about the schedule – even when Lucy was moved out of the nursing home into what everyone else called 'sheltered accommodation', but seemed to me to be no more than a house full of weirdos. Along with them came a procession of 'minders' who always seemed to get first pick of any biscuits going begging, and who infuriated Natasha with their habit of cheerfully stepping over all the empty drink cans scattered around as if the messiness of those sad souls was nothing much to do with them.

But they were patient and kind, and put a deal of effort into things they must have reckoned more important than being tidy. They never ever forgot a name – not even of the visitors, like me, who came so rarely. They celebrated all the inmates' – sorry, *clients*' – birthdays, and took them on day trips. They held a lot of special parties for things like Halloween and Bonfire Night, to which I got some strangely illustrated invitations done by the biggest weirdo of them all, who was called 'Box'. ('You ought to keep those clean and safe,' Natasha told me. 'I am *serious*. I think they could be very valuable one day.')

So off we went, once every twelve weeks, with no more arguments. I think that I was ticking off the visits in my mind. Nothing was said, but generally, I noticed, we stayed an hour and twenty minutes, which I put down to Nicholas reckoning that was the shortest decent amount of time a son could spend with his mother. A moment after that, he would be glancing casually at his watch and saying things like, 'Lucy, I wonder if you'd mind if I snatched Eddie away now. There are a couple of things I really ought to do when I get back.'

She'd smile. (She smiled at *everything*. Sometimes I thought that being away from Harris had been enough to make all of her days a simple joy. And sometimes I thought she was just simple.) Nicholas would move behind to give me a tiny push. I'd force myself to smile more warmly and move close to hug her. She would cling to me. Nicholas would wait a moment before prising me away. 'So sorry, Lucy. Must take him from you. But we'll see you soon.'

With one or two closed doors, and one last nod at whichever minder was in the kitchen today, we would be out at last.

Then one day Alice changed everything. As I was clambering resignedly into the car, she asked, 'Can I come too?'

I didn't think she could have realized where Nicholas and I were going. 'We're off to see my mum.'

'So?'

'Why would you want to come?'

'Because she's your mother, you dim bulb. And I've never met her.' Through the car window she appealed to Nicholas. 'That's all right, isn't it? I mean, it's *nice* that I want to meet someone from Edward's family.'

Nicholas was clearly stumped. 'I suppose it's up to Edward.' He turned to me. 'What do you think?'

I shrugged, embarrassed to the core. I'd rather have been staked out as a meal for fire ants than have Alice meet my mother. But she had asked nicely enough, and it was hard to say no to what sounded like a reasonable request.

So I said yes, and Alice dived into the car, not even arguing about her right to the front seat. (As I'd got bolder about 'turns', she'd changed the grounds of her demand, claiming that she got carsick.) Usually on the way to Ivy House I had to suffer Nicholas's delicate remarks about how much these visits meant to Lucy, and

136

how glad I'd be 'later on' that I had kept them up. (The first, I doubted. And the second I, no doubt correctly, took to mean 'after her death'.)

With Alice in the car, things were quite different. She started off complaining about some joker in her class at school. She interrupted herself to accuse Nicholas of gross hypocrisy for moaning about another driver using his mobile phone while he himself was speeding. Then she told several rather good jokes and, after that, began complaining about her school again.

And we were there! I couldn't quite believe it. I'd no idea the journey could seem so short.

As ever, Nicholas was full of tact. 'All right, Edward? Any second thoughts? Because I can easily wait in the garden with Alice.'

The garden was often filled with weirdos anyhow. And they had been good jokes. So I said, 'No. Alice can come.'

So Alice came. And she was *wonderful*, friendly and easy-going with everyone. She shook hands with the minders. She gave the massive woman who grins at everyone as if they are her best friend a big hug. She had a really long chat with one of the most awkward of the loonies, agreeing he could probably use the power of his mind to fetch down planes. She stepped over Box's naked spread-eagled legs with such calm grace that you'd have thought he'd sat himself down on the floor in that hall-way simply to act as a doormat in case she wanted to

wipe her feet, and not in order to draw some giant cobweb high on the wall.

And when we found my mother, Alice actually made
her laugh. I don't know how she did it. Afterwards, I
asked Nicholas more than once, 'What did she *say*? You
were there! What *was* it Alice said that set my mum off,
not just carrying on with that weird smile, but really
giggling?' But he could not remember either. All we know
is that we went in the room and within minutes my
mother – my mother! – was flirting and giggling: flirting
with Alice and giggling at her jokes and flip remarks.
Except in my most early memories – and they were
blurred – I couldn't recall my mother seeming so much
in the same world as everyone around her. When
Nicholas said, 'Hey, Alice! If we don't get back on the
road soon, you're going to miss your tennis lesson,' I was
astonished.

We'd been there over two hours.

Alice flung her arms round my mum and hugged her.
Smacking a giant kiss onto her cheek, she told her
cheerily, 'Bye, Lucy! See you soon.'

I copied her. 'Bye, Mum.'

Mum squeezed my hand. I think she might not have
remembered my name because there was a sort of
choking gap after the word 'goodbye'. But in a moment
we were out of there, and Alice was bouncing down the
gravel path towards the car. 'That was good fun.'

Nicholas slid his arm round her shoulders, maybe to

calm her down, and maybe to make her listen when he said, 'I'm really glad that you came with us, Alice. You were *brilliant.*'

I felt there was a moment, just before we reached the car, when it was my turn to say something grateful. But I couldn't think of what to say. How do you thank a person for teaching you that your own mother can be hugged?

Alice just grinned and took the front seat without asking, knowing full well she'd earned it. Nicholas gave her a moment more to settle down, and then he said again, 'Alice, my lovely, you were such a hit in there. All of them *loved* you.'

He'd given me my chance. 'Especially my mum. You even made her laugh.'

'Your mum's dead easy,' Alice said.

And, after that day, suddenly she was.

Nicholas

I'm going to be honest. I would have loved some children of my own. I'd have had cotfuls. When we found out Natasha was infertile, I was so deeply shocked and disappointed that I dared not show it.

She too had always thought in terms of having a big family. That weird upbringing of hers had made her envy all the friends who'd grown up carelessly sprawling across their kitchen tables, and arguing back when someone told them off for leaving clutter about or playing music too loud.

Not that Natasha ever wanted to run a household like that. No, what she wanted was the warmth – the sheer normality – of having children about. She cried for days after we got the news.

But she is not the sort to crumble under any blow. She's a go-getter. And as months passed, the notion of giving someone else's child a proper home appealed more and more. Alice, of course, as good as fell into our lap. Natasha knew her mother from visits to the clinic. (Natasha was given bad news but, as she was only too well aware, Tamara was given worse.) Alice began to spend more and more time at our house. We passed the social workers' tests. She was adopted legally. So we were three.

Before we took on Alice, I don't believe Natasha had the faintest idea how much sheer time and effort is involved in raising a child. And she was happy at work. We asked for a second adoption mostly because of Alice. (You don't say that to social workers, of course. In fact, there's scarcely anything that you can say to them that passes muster. In my more irritated moments, I've thought that they're hair-triggered to be suspicious of any normal reason for wanting a child.)

Rob came round several times before we took on Eddie. (I still think of that pale, unconfident child who first moved in with us as 'Eddie'.) Rob warned us that there could – no, that there probably *would* – be troubles ahead. 'He seems to have come out of things almost too well. There may be repercussions.' He said, so far as they could tell, Eddie's first years must have been fairly stable. His personality was strong, and he could form attachments. But childhood's not a cakewalk, and all these kids face added stress by virtue of the things that they've been through. 'So we can never be sure what's going to happen.'

That's true of any child. Nobody can foretell the future. Natasha felt as I did, that Eddie would have his best chance in our house. With us.

Alice was keen. It worked out better than expected. And every time I saw his hopeless mother in that ghastly place of hers, I blessed the day Rob Reed phoned up and said, 'Is there a time this week I could come round to talk to you and your wife? You see, something's come up.'

Why did we call him Edward? Well, to be frank, it was because Natasha can't stand shortened names. You'll notice that she calls me Nicholas. (So do the children.) She won't admit that, since it sounds like snobbery, so she pretends she had a horrid boyfriend once, called Eddie. Everyone understands that sort of thing can put you off a name.

He grew in confidence as well as height. Gradually he stopped tensing up so horribly each time he heard a key scrape in a lock, or a bolt shoot across. That made him easier to love, of course – that vulnerability, that sense of his grim past still hovering over him.

That is the problem with these kids, of course. Whatever pain or loss it was that made them come to you, that never goes. It's always there. Always. There in the background like a lurking enemy, waiting to trip them up.

Or worse, waiting for them to trip themselves.

Eddie

My school might not have been as classy as the one Alice was sent to, but it was good at trips. It seemed to me that every other week a gang of us would pile into a minibus. Off we'd go, mucking about till one of the teachers stood up to tell us to behave ourselves. At last we'd settle down – until we reached wherever it was. A railway museum. An art gallery. A country meadow where no one had ever used a single chemical, crazy with flowers. Once we went off to see some iron bridge famous for something I've forgotten. Longest this. Highest that. Whatever. All I remember is how black and sturdy the thing looked, towering above us, and how annoyed we were when we were told that we'd be staying underneath.

As we got older, most of the trips became more dull, almost as if the teachers who arranged them were trying to warn us where we might end up if we didn't knuckle down. We went to some enormous book storage hangar where giant robot arms picked out dull, tightly wrapped packages, and men and women in overalls scuttled along the stacks, sorting out what they called 'glitches'. I missed the trip to the cosmetics factory. (Alice was livid with me since she'd known I had copped out that morning, pretending to feel sicker than I was, and everyone came home with buckets of free stuff for mums and sisters.)

Then, one day, we were divided into even smaller groups. It was a visit to the university, and we were dropped off outside different buildings. Department of Engineering. Modern Studies. Fine Art. Mine was the very last group to leave the bus. Our building didn't even have a name outside, but in the hall there were some animal skeletons in large glass cases, like in a museum.

The five of us trooped up the stairs behind a girl in a white coat who had the longest ponytail I'd ever seen. Her name, she told us, was Stefania, and though her English sounded perfect to me she had an accent someone whispered was Romanian or Russian. She led us down a drab green corridor into a long laboratory which stank of some strange minty chemical.

She told us what it was, but I've forgotten.

Then we went through another set of swinging doors. Stefania told us we were now in Palaeoanthropology, and we had such a noisy laugh about that that she spun round and rather fiercely made us chant it about ten times over, till we could say it properly. (I still can.) The people there were working with fragments of bone. Some were spread out in separate rough circles, like jigsaw bits sorted before you start a puzzle. Some were just heaped in trays. At first, Stefania was interesting, talking about the things you could work out from faces. I do remember her telling us Neanderthal man's great massive brow ridge (she had to explain to Justin which bit of the face she meant) was there to make him look even more threatening when he glared.

But most of it was way, way duller than that, and I stopped listening and wandered further along the bench.

Suddenly she broke off. 'Ah,' she said. 'I see you're making for our answer to *Time Team*!'

I didn't even know what she was talking about, so I just grinned.

She herded everyone along and through the next set of doors. 'This is so clever. You see, we take the final bone structure, so far as we can get the jigsaw right. And then we build up on top – muscles and flesh. And there are often clues to hair and eye colour to do with different racial characteristics.'

Justin's not very bright. He only had to hear the word 'racial' to flick at Tyrrell's dreadlocks. Tyrrell played up, and proudly took a bow while we all cheered and jeered.

Stefania looked a bit put out. Perhaps they didn't have our sort of teasing in Romania. But she pressed on. 'Of course, you can't get it absolutely right. But you can make a really good attempt at knowing what these people looked like.'

That's when I realized some of the bits of bone must have been human.

'But what's the point?' Tina asked mardily.

Stefania was astonished. 'What's the *point*? Well, it's just finding out! Don't you want to find out things? Aren't you interested in things around you?'

'There aren't any old bones around *me*,' smirked Tina.

You could tell Stefania was irritated. It was as if Tina had said that she was wasting her life, and her enthusiasm for the bones was stupid. She bit her lip and looked back though the glass swing doors into the other laboratory. The two who had been working at the bench when we trooped past had disappeared.

'Right, then,' she said, as if she'd suddenly made a big decision. 'I'll show you one way that this work is useful.'

She used a key to unlock a small box on the wall. Inside were more keys. Lifting one off its hook, she relocked the box, and led us through another door I hadn't even noticed. 'No one's to touch a thing in here! Not a thing!'

You could tell she was deadly serious, and we fell silent and watched as she pulled open a filing-cabinet drawer to take out a file. On top, there was a photo of a small boy. It was as if the mere sight of his face made her have second thoughts about sharing what she had planned. At once she shoved the file back in the cabinet, then reached up to a shelf above her head for a large old-fashioned Polaroid camera.

I was the one she nodded at. 'Stand still. Don't smile.'

I was too startled even to think of smiling. The shutter clattered down. There was a winding sound. 'Two minutes. Just two minutes.'

While we were waiting, she opened up some fancy scanner. I drifted off to look at the cartoons someone had pinned on a cork board. Most of them seemed to be about archaeologists and their dug-up bones. I didn't get some of the jokes.

When I came back, the others were leaning over a computer, staring at the screen. Even Tina seemed out of her bad mood.

I started listening to Stefania again.

'. . . because the facial bones grow in proportion, and other features tend to stay the same. So, as with the fragments next door, the programme puts two and two together and does a really good job of working out how any missing child might look as the years pass.'

'Edward's not missing.'

'No, he's not. But if he were, and we didn't find him for ten years, we would still have an excellent idea of what he'd look like.'

She pressed a few more keys. Tina and Martin moved aside to let me in to look.

And there, staring out from the computer screen, unsmiling as ever, was Bryce Harris.

I don't know how long I was on the floor. I was told after

that Stefania thought I'd had a fit. She was just asking everyone if it had happened before, and whether they knew if she should call an ambulance, when I came round.

I hadn't even *realized* then. I mean, the shock of seeing Harris's face was what had done for me. They helped me back onto my feet.

Stefania offered a lifeline. 'Did you miss your breakfast?'

I nodded, acting gormless, and took the tea and biscuits that she offered me. I was too busy making sure I didn't mention Harris to let my thoughts drift further, and it was only on the bus, halfway home, that the point really struck me.

That was *my* face, grown ten years older.

I had Harris's face.

I must have looked as pale as death when I walked in. Nicholas would have noticed at once, but I was lucky. It was Natasha in the kitchen. I scuttled past her, muttering something about being 'desperate', and rushed upstairs to lock myself in the bathroom.

After a minute or two she was concerned enough to come up after me and tap on the door. 'Edward? Are you all right?'

'I'm fine,' I said. 'Sorry about the rush. Out in a moment.'

I heard her footsteps fade along the landing, and

dropped my head between my knees again, the way that I'd been taught. I was so rattled I forgot to pee. And after I'd come down again a few minutes later to say hello properly, I saw Natasha glance at me curiously when, without thinking, I went off to the downstairs loo.

'Are you *sure* you're all right?' she asked when I came out. 'You're looking awfully peaky.'

'I'm fine. Really, I'm fine.'

Supper was early because Natasha had to supervise some fancy evening event. Nicholas came home shattered from three site visits in a row, and so we were a quiet group around the table that night. Nicholas asked Alice about her awful day. (She hated Wednesdays. All of the things she loathed the most, or couldn't do, happened on Wednesdays.)

And then he turned to me. 'What about you?'

I couldn't tell them I'd spent most of the day trying to force Bryce Harris's face out of my mind. 'Me?' I said. 'Oh, we had a trip to a yarn factory.'

Even as it popped out, I found myself thinking, *Where did* that *come from?* But I remembered at once. It was a visit we had made with Mr Perkins.

Nicholas made a face. 'A *yarn* factory?'

Was he suspicious? No. Alice was smiling broadly, but whether that was because she thought the idea was amusing, or whether she knew that I was lying, it was impossible to tell.

'What was it like?' Nicholas asked dutifully.

And off I went, describing it in just the same way that Mr Perkins had. I talked about the spindles, and the complicated way the yarn was threaded so it didn't pull so tightly it kept snapping. I talked of where the various yarns came from, and how they were dyed in giant vats and each batch was called a 'dye lot' with its own special number because, if you were making something, it was important to make sure all your yarn came from the same dye lot. If not, the shade of colour might be just a tiny bit different.

I only stopped myself in time from echoing Mr Perkins's enthusiastic cry of, 'All the colours of the rainbow – and more!'

Once I'd begun, I couldn't rein myself in. I talked about great lorries backing up to the unloading bays, and how crates of the yarn were sent to stockists all over the world.

My voice trailed off at last. Alice was watching me closely. Natasha's thoughts were clearly miles away, probably trawling through the complications of her coming evening. And I had bored Nicholas almost to death.

'Sounds good,' he said.

'Well,' I said, trying to backtrack into acting a bit more normal, 'it was pretty boring really.'

'Still . . .'

Stifling a yawn, Nicholas rose from the table. 'Better get on with things.'

He turned to Natasha. 'What was it that you said you needed out of the loft?'

'Just the old tripod. Malcolm's won't clamp any more, and his new one hasn't arrived yet.'

Usually Nicholas managed on his own. This time, perhaps because he was so tired, he asked me, 'Want to go up?'

I'd never been up in the loft before, and I was curious. Nicholas held the ladder. It took a bit of time to find the tripod because it was stored away in a red cover no one had thought to mention. I slid it over to the hatch, and just as Nicholas reached up to take it, banged my knee on the corner of a box. 'Yee-*ouch*!'

His head popped through. 'Hurt yourself?'

I pointed. 'What *is* that? Is it an old TV and *video* player?'

I saw him blush. 'It was for you,' he said. 'When you first came, I thought that you might want to play those ancient tapes of yours. That's why it's here.'

Would I have wanted to watch them anyway? Or was it just because I'd felt so close to Mr Perkins all through supper?

'So can we get it down?'

'What, *now*?'

'Why not? I'm up here. You're down there.'

Already I was pushing it towards the hatch. I watched him wondering whether or not to argue. Then, with a sigh, he pulled the ladder back to form a better angle and we slid it down.

'It might not work,' he warned.

'I'll put it in my room,' I said. 'Out of the way.'

We both knew what that meant: somewhere the sheer boxiness of it would not annoy Natasha.

On the floor of my cupboard.

The moment Nicholas had gone after saying goodnight, Alice was in my doorway. 'What was all *that* about?'

'All what?'

'You know.' She shut the door behind her. 'All of that crap about a yarn factory. Justin told me that your lot went to look at some manky old bones.'

That startled me. 'So how come you know Justin?'

She brushed my question aside. 'Never mind that. How come you told them all that rubbish at supper?'

'It didn't *matter*,' I said defensively. 'Neither of them was listening anyway.'

'Who would?' She snorted with contempt. 'Spindles and shuttles and twists and vat lots and stuff.'

'*Dye* lots.'

'Who cares?' She dropped down on the rug in front of me, and spun the measuring tape that I'd been fiddling with away across the floor, out of my reach. 'Why were you telling all those stupid lies? Justin says you've been acting weird all day. He says you fainted at the university, and didn't even hear when people got at you on the way home.'

'Got at me?' (I was baffled.)

151

'Teased you because you'll grow into someone so ugly not even you can look at yourself without collapsing.'

'I didn't even *hear* them.'

'That's what he said. He said you were pale as a grub, and on a different planet. He said—' She broke off. 'Edward, are you *crying*?'

I suppose I must have been.

She shuffled nearer. 'God, *sorry*, Eddie. I didn't mean to come in here and upset you. I just wanted to know what happened. You know – why you were so odd at supper.'

That frightened me. 'Do you think that they noticed?'

Alice shrugged. 'Not sure. But you'll be down before they see you again.'

'Down?'

'From whatever you took.'

'I haven't taken anything.'

She grinned. 'Oh, yes, and pigs can fly.'

'No, really.'

Now she was getting ratty. 'Come off it, Ed! You should have *seen* yourself. Eyes glittering, with all that rubbish about wool and wefts and warps and stuff tumbling out of your mouth at five hundred miles an hour. I am amazed they didn't notice. You were dead lucky that Natasha wasn't listening, and Nicholas was half asleep.' She leaned in closer. 'Come on, Ed. I thought that we were *mates*. Somebody must have given you *something*. So tell me.'

'Nobody gave me anything! I just saw Harris!'

'Harris?'

'You know.' Already I could feel myself shrivelling on the rug. 'Bryce Harris! That man who lived with us – me and my mum.'

'Oh, *him*! The Beast!'

'The Beast?'

'That's what we called him – well, that's what *I* called him.' She saw my baffled look. 'They had to *warn* me,' she explained. 'Before you came. They had to explain a bit about the mean stuff that had happened to you in your life, in case you acted weird.' She laid her fingers on mine, but only to stop me picking threads out of the rug. 'I don't know if they ever said he was called Harris. I know it was definitely me who called him the Beast because I remember Nicholas nodding and saying, "That's about it." And the name sort of stuck.'

'I never heard you say it.'

She said with scorn, 'Why would you? I certainly knew better than to mention him in front of *you*.' She waited for a moment, then she said, 'Why, is he out?'

'Of prison? How should I know?'

'You said you *saw* him.'

And again I did. The image swooped at me. 'No!' I almost shouted. (Later she told me I was flapping my hands in front of me, as if to brush moths away.) 'I saw his *face*.'

'Sssh! Keep it down!'

But I'd collapsed into a flood of tears and snivelling.

She dug a heap of tissues out of the box on my shelf and sat cross-legged, waiting for me to stop my sobbing long enough to tell her what had happened. As soon as she had understood, she tried to comfort me. 'That doesn't mean that Harris is your *dad*! He might simply be some uncle or cousin, or even someone who just happens to look a bit like you'll look when you're older.'

I must have given her a look of utter disbelief because she pressed on hotly, 'What's wrong with that? Everyone tells me I look like Natasha.'

'No, they don't. Only Mrs Joy. And Nicholas says that she only says it because she's about a hundred years old and thinks it's a way of being nice, and making you feel better about being adopted.'

She hit back. 'All right. So maybe Harris *is* your real dad. You can see why your mother gave you a different name and made you think he wasn't.'

But perhaps she hadn't. When I tried thinking about it, I had no idea how I first came to be so sure that Harris was not my father. I couldn't remember anything said by my mum, or snarled by Harris, about my being anyone else's child.

Alice gave up on watching me struggle to remember. 'I know,' she said. 'Next time we visit, I can have a go at asking Lucy for you.'

I didn't bother to respond. After all, both of us knew my mother couldn't even say for sure if she took sugar in her tea.

She took a different tack. 'Or you could ask Natasha and Nicholas if you can have one of those DNA tests.'

Through my brain rushed one terrifying scene after another. A mix-up with letters so Harris saw my new name and address. Harris phoning the health centre and somehow finding out my own appointment time.

Basically, Harris finding me.

All that I said to Alice was, 'I think I'd rather not know.'

She shrugged, 'Well, even if he *is* your dad, that doesn't mean that you'll be anything like him. Look at me! My mother never told me anything about my father. For all I know he was a serial *axe* murderer or something. Having a rotten mum or dad is not the worst thing in the world. Hundreds of people must have them.' She thought for a moment. 'Millions, actually. All over the world.'

I must have been crying again by then, because she jumped to her feet. 'Wait here! Don't move! I'm going to fetch you something to cheer you up.'

'What?'

But she was gone, across the landing, back to her own room.

It can't have been more than a minute before she was back. And as she scuttled through my door again, holding her school bag, she asked me, 'What have you got to block it?'

'Block what?'

'The *door*, dummy!' Already she was looking in my cupboard. 'This'll do.' Dragging out the big square box

155

I'd pushed in there less than an hour before, she rammed it up against the door.

'You sit on it,' she ordered.

'Why?'

'Safer.' Out of her pocket, she pulled a twist of paper. 'Here, have one of these. It'll make you feel better.'

The truth is that I didn't clock what she was giving me. The only thing I recognized was the bright can she pulled out of her bag and offered me so I could wash the pill down. It was one of those shiny ring-pull affairs they sell at corner shops and railway stations: bright, chirpy alcoholic drinks with cheerful Friday-night names like Whisky Kick, Vodka Fizz and Gin Whirl.

I'd had a sip of almost every gin and tonic Nicholas had ever poured for himself, and sometimes more if he had left the room. (Natasha hardly ever drank. She said she'd seen enough pools of vomit on her expensive glossy marquee floors to put her off booze for life.) I'd never had a proper drink all to myself. I must have glugged it down because even Alice warned, 'Hey! Steady on!' and, as I found out later, she had been throwing these things back for ages – since she fell in with one of Justin's brothers at a friend's party.

I gave her back the empty can so she could stow it out of sight, away in the bottom of her school bag.

'Better?'

I nodded. 'Nice warm feeling. Tingly toes.'

'That's not the Tequila Tang. That is the bluey kicking in.'

'The bluey?'

'What I gave you.'

'That pill? I thought that was an aspirin.'

'Eddie, you're such a *nerd*.'

Now I was grinning too. We shared a silly conversation about my yarn about the yarn factory. (I thought that was a *hoot*.) And then it started. It was the weirdest feeling, as if each muscle in my face was part of a giant cobweb, throbbing pleasantly behind a shell of warm skin. Even as I was liking that, the warmth spread down. I hadn't realized that my stomach was a knot until it loosened. You would have thought someone had opened a trap door in my heels, and all the misery and upset was dropping through to leave room for this warmth and light and happiness to take its place, all through my body. Somehow the two of us changed places, Alice and I, and she was sitting on the box to guard the door, and I was back on the rug, feeling myself spin in the gentlest of cradles, with strangely glimmering colours sheeting through my brain, while what had been the usual boring drumming of rain against the window panes had turned into the sound of magical bells.

'Edward, don't drop off in your clothes!'

'Sorry?'

'You're practically *asleep*.'

'Am I?' I opened my eyes, surprised to find myself staring at the ceiling, and not the wall. 'How long have I been lying down?'

'Ages. Natasha will be back. I'd better go.'

'Thanks for the—' I'd no idea what it was called. 'Thanks for the stuff.'

Alice gave me the most beautiful smile. 'You're welcome.' Behind her skin and hair and all those colours she rubbed around her eyes, I saw her as she must have been when she was four or five years old, open to anything, ready to clown around, eager and keen.

'You look so *young*,' I told her, filled with wonder.

'I *am* young.'

It really mattered that she understood. 'No, Alice, I am *serious*. You suddenly look about *five*. All glowing, like a happy angel.'

She blew a kiss at me – not anything soppy, just a friendly gesture. 'Have a good trip!' she said. 'Be happy, Edward.'

She pushed the video box aside, and shimmered out.

It was a pretty primitive machine. Plug in. Switch on. Self-tune. I'd lost my sense of time, but still it couldn't have been more than a couple of minutes before the clicking and the whirring stopped.

I didn't want to miss a single moment, so I leaned forward to rewind. The machine chugged back to the start, and I pressed Play. The picture settled and the jaunty music that I knew so well burst out upon the room. I stabbed the volume button till it was much quieter. I didn't need it loud. The tune swam in my head.

I don't know what I'd thought would happen. Perhaps I'd feared I would fall straight back into being that pale child who Rob found cowering against the wall. Perhaps I'd thought I'd sit with a smirk on my face, astonished that even my much younger self could have been so entranced by some old duffer in a cardigan with leather buttons.

What I'd not reckoned on was this third child. This *stranger* who, as Mr Perkins backed in through the door, shaking the drops from his umbrella and turning to catch my eyes with his warm, fatherly smile, whispered to him so happily, 'Hi, Mr Perkins.'

I actually heard myself say it. I felt myself shunt closer across the rug, till Mr Perkins was so near to me he almost blurred. I felt myself mouthing the words I knew by heart. '*Hello. My, it's so cold and rainy out there today! But we're warm and cosy in here. So shall we sing our song together?*'

And we did.

> '*Happy days, and happy ways*
> *I hope you know how glad I am*
> *To see you here with me today*
> *We're going to have great fun.*'

It was the trip to the pet show. Even before he told us I knew that, the way that if you've listened to a set of songs often enough in the same order, what's coming next is always ringing in your brain before the first chords start. He filled the kettle and fed Sooty-Sue as usual, all the while talking to us about responsibility – about not pestering our parents to give us living creatures we wouldn't be able to keep well and happy. 'A pet should never be one person's present,' he told us gravely. 'They have to be a wanted member of the whole family. They are a lot of work, and need a good deal of attention. So everyone in the household has to agree.'

Then we went off to see the children who showed us their pets. I hadn't forgotten any. I still knew all their names, even before he introduced us again. Then, when they'd showed us how they cleaned out a rabbit hutch, or fetched hay for their pony, or made a hibernation box so that their tortoise would be warm and safe through the winter, he drew us in. 'See? These children here have learned all sorts of skills to keep their pets happy and well. And we can also be good at looking after all the animals we meet, even if it is only being kind to the cat next door, or remembering to take a carrot to the horse we pass on our Sunday walk.'

He smiled. 'Let's sing our song about learning to do things, shall we?'

I sang along with him, the way I always had.

'Some things seem very hard to do
You think you won't be able
To get them right,

But then you do
And you win through
Because you're strong and brave inside
But most of all, of course, because you want to,
Want to, want to.
Because you're strong and brave inside
And really, really want to.'

All the time we were singing, he was on his way back to his house, swinging his bright umbrella. He checked the stick insect inside the jar ('About the easiest pet you can keep.') and stroked Sooty-Sue while he kept chatting about other animals. Then he put on his jacket and picked up his umbrella again. 'It's *still* raining! Never mind. I have a good feeling that it'll be much sunnier next time we meet. I'll see you then, shall I?'

Again, I heard myself whispering, 'Yes.'

He looked me full in the face. His eyes were twinkling – full of fun and love. 'Goodbye,' he said. 'Try to be happy.'

'Goodbye,' I whispered. 'Goodbye, Mr Perkins. Goodbye, Dad.'

III

Edward

I've no idea why it ate in to me so badly, the realization that Harris and I must be blood family. As Alice pointed out, pretty well everyone has a bad sheep or two among their relations somewhere, and even those like her who don't know any details can't bank on them not being there simply because of that. I'd seen enough on telly and in the newspapers to know that Harris wasn't by any means the foulest person around. He was a bully and a drunk. He was a horrible man. He didn't care about a single soul except himself. And he was violent.

But there are worse about.

It's just I didn't want to be anything to do with him – not simply in my day-to-day life, but in any way at all. He was the man who'd kicked my mother about, and beaten her simple, and I was desperate for there to be no link between us at all. Why should I want this monster muscling in and spoiling things in my mind when, from the start it seems, I had already chosen kind, gentle Mr Perkins as my real father?

And Eleanor Holdenbach must have realized that. Once, on my way back sooner than expected from the lavatory along from her office, I'd overheard her saying to Rob: 'That Mr Perkins has been a life-saver.' The memory stuck because I'd been surprised that she knew anything about Mr Perkins, apart from what I'd told her. She'd claimed she'd never watched his show, so how would she have known what I, who'd spent a thousand hours in his company, had never known – that he must once have rescued someone who was in desperate straits?

I hadn't realized she'd been talking of me.

So perhaps, when things took such a nosedive after the visit to the university, I should have had the sense to ask to see her again. They'd always, all of them, kept saying through the years, 'Edward, if ever you should feel the need to talk to someone . . .' Always I'd tuned out at once. Bleh, bleh. Bleh, bleh. And why should I have felt the need? I had been happy enough.

But now I found things going wrong. *Haunted* was what I felt. Between me and whatever I was looking at – a set of questions in a school test, something on television, even a soaring football – Harris's face would suddenly appear. Sometimes his look was threatening. Sometimes he wore that smirk I knew so well, or that grim look of concentration that used to spread across his face whenever he hurled me aside and set about my mum.

'Edward? Edward Stead, are you paying attention?'

Each teacher in turn lost patience. But how could I explain, without letting on who I'd once been, and who I dreaded to be? Nicholas begged me, 'What is the *matter*, Edward? The school's at its wits' end with you this term. What's on your mind?'

I couldn't tell him either, though for the life of me I don't know why. So on I struggled, restless and nervous, lying awake at nights and snapping at everyone. Time and again, I saw Natasha seek out Nicholas's eyes across the supper table. '*You* deal with him,' her face said, plain as paint. 'I've had enough.'

Alice stopped teasing me — a sure sign that our partnership was under strain. Sometimes I caught her watching me, a worried look on her face. And then one evening, after a meal studded with Natasha's increasingly irritated scoldings, Nicholas's tired pleas and my unhelpful snarls, she came into my room.

I didn't make things easy. 'What do *you* want?'

'Now, now! Miss Manners wouldn't think that was a very nice welcome.'

'Just push off, Alice.'

'No. I want to talk to you.'

'Well, I don't want to talk to you.'

She made a face. 'So tell me something new. You don't want to talk to *anyone*.'

'No, I don't.' I thought of adding, 'Especially not to you.' But even to me, that sounded far too childish.

By now she'd hitched up her school skirt and slid

herself onto my table. She threw one leg across the other as if she knew that such a grown-up, feminine pose would stop me trying to manhandle her out of the room the way I might have done before. 'What has got into you, Eddie? You're being horrible to everyone.'

'I'm all right so long as everyone leaves me alone.'

'You're not, though. You're a mess. And Justin says that all your teachers think you're going to fail your exams.'

'It's none of Justin's business. Or yours.'

Now she was leaning forward. 'But it *is*, though, isn't it? Because all this is my fault. It was me who started you off.'

'Started me off?'

'With the bluey.'

'The bluey?'

'Yes. That was the first you'd had, wasn't it?'

Now I remembered. She was talking of the pill she'd given me so many weeks before.

She'd started up again. 'And now you're clearly on to something else. So it's my fault. I shouldn't ever have given you anything that night. I feel so *guilty*. I don't know what you're on, or where you're getting it. But it's not doing you any good and I think you should stop.' Her cheeks were pink now. 'In fact, I think that you should probably stop trying to deal with all this in your own screwed-up head. You ought to go downstairs right now and ask to talk to Nicholas on his own, and tell him all about that stupid Bryce Harris computer picture, and what's been happening.'

'*Nothing's* been happening!'

'Come off it, Eddie! Anyone in the world could look at you and know you're taking something!'

'I'm *not*!'

'That's almost proof.' Her voice brimmed with pure scorn. 'All druggies lie through their teeth.'

'I'm not a druggie!'

Alice raised her palms. 'OK, OK! You're not a druggie. I believe you. Honestly I do.'

It was the sheer contempt with which she said it that made me spring across to tug her hair so hard I pulled her off the table. She stumbled to her feet, then turned, eyes glittering with tears of pain.

'Oh, *right*!' she said. 'Who did you learn that nasty trick from, Eddie? Could it have been your very own real dad, *Bryce Harris*?'

She told, of course. Oh, not about the hair-pulling or what she thought was going on with drugs. She doubled back from school the very next morning, missing her favourite lessons, in order to tell Nicholas about my visit to the university, and what I'd said about the face on the computer. 'That's why he's like he is. He thinks that he'll turn into Harris.'

Nicholas reported all this back to me, along with a stern lecture about the fact that I was not to pick on Alice for breaking a confidence. She'd done what she thought best, and he would hope that if my sister ever found herself in the same state, I'd do the same for her.

I knew exactly what he meant. I also knew I would. If Alice had been halfway as messed up and miserable as I was, I would have rushed to get his help.

But somehow I couldn't say that. I couldn't say a single thing that was normal or sensible. All I could do was snarl, 'I am not "in a state". I just want to be left *alone*.'

'Oh, come on, Edward. That man has spoiled enough of other people's lives. And more than enough of yours. Here you were, doing beautifully. Everyone said so. Everyone was astonished at how well you've been managing over the years. This is a setback, I admit. We'll have to face it.' He sank down on my bed. 'First, of course, we will need the facts.'

'Oh, yes?' I said sarcastically. 'Track Harris down and ask him if he'd mind taking a DNA test?'

Nicholas seemed surprised I'd thought even this far along the path. How could he know that every living minute of mine had been chewed up with thoughts of how I could find out the truth. *Was* Harris my father? Or was he merely an uncle or a cousin of some sort? Maybe it was pure coincidence that we looked alike. After all, everyone in the world has types they fancy. Perhaps my mother had always been attracted to men with Harris's build and facial features?

Maybe I was the child of one of them, not him.

170

Nicholas ran his fingers through his thinning hair. 'Natasha and I are going to have to think about all this. And maybe talk to Rob.'

'Throw them all in,' I said sarcastically. 'Don't forget that policewoman Sue, and Eleanor Holdenbach. And maybe that nurse who cut my toenails at the hospital. And of course Linda and Alan.'

'All people who *care* about you! And it's quite a list!'

I should have felt ashamed. I think I did. But not enough to draw back and apologize. I was in *pain*. I didn't know what to do or what to say, and all the time my brain was spinning with the misery of having even the shadow of bloody Harris looming over me.

Perhaps for ever.

I got so near to begging Nicholas to send me back to Eleanor Holdenbach. She would have understood. But then I suddenly remembered all the questions – how they had driven me so close to crazy, on and on and on. First Rob, then Sue, then Eleanor. Questions and questions and questions. Over and over and over.

I couldn't bear to think of going through all that again.

Nicholas was clearly waiting for me to say something. But I stared at the floor. I couldn't think of anything that might help him feel better. I couldn't think of anything to help myself.

In the end, sighing, Nicholas pushed his hands down on his knees to lever himself up from the bed. 'I see we're going to get nowhere tonight. Let's leave it, Edward. We will have time to think about what's best for you, and you'll have time to think about what you want too.'

His hand came down on my shoulder. 'I am so sorry that this happened. It was such bad luck. If they had only chosen someone else to photograph!'

Did he believe I hadn't thought of that? That I'd not thrashed around in bed, exhausted with the effort of telling myself, 'That's all you have to do. Pretend that it was someone else Stefania chose when she picked up the camera. Tina, or Martin, or Justin. Anyone. It didn't have to be you. So just pretend it wasn't. Put it out of your mind. Then you can go on just the way you were before. After all, nothing has changed. So what's the point in letting these weird thoughts chew you up all day, all night? Let them go, Eddie! Let them go! Forget the whole damn thing!'

On and on. Telling myself all night. Most of the day.

And always hopeless. Absolutely hopeless. The thing is, I'd begun to see him everywhere. My heart would thump. I would creep up to sneak a look and ask myself afterwards, 'How could I even have *begun to think* that could be him?' I'd realize that it was because the man was wearing the same sort of jacket Harris did, or had his knuckles clenched. Something as simple as that.

And now I knew that I was going to look like him.

I had proof too. One dark December evening, Natasha sent me on the bus to pick up something she had left at work. Just papers, but she needed them and Malcolm was working in the office until late.

Some great fat woman took the seat beside me. There were some places free, but she was probably too heavy on her feet to bother moving further along the bus. She squashed me up against the window frame. I can remember what was in my mind. I sat there wondering if she had children who were dead embarrassed when she came waddling into school. In fact, I can remember feeling lucky my own mum was so hidden away.

And then this woman shifted in her seat. I had a horror she was going to talk to me, and anyone who got on at the following stops might think we were together. So I turned away.

Harris was gazing at me.

I couldn't budge. I was wedged in. In any case, I realized instantly he wasn't there – that it was only my own face warped to look strained and old, the way that faces do when they're reflected in bus windows in the dark and wet.

Still, it was Harris again.

Nicholas

We did our best. And after all, it wasn't as if we didn't know what was the matter with him. Alice astonished me by taking charge of one part of the problem. Without a word to me, she engineered things so that Edward left his mother's room in Ivy House to fetch a cake she claimed was in the car. (He never hurried back from any errand that could get him out of there for a few minutes.)

The moment Edward shut the door behind him, Alice asked Lucy outright:

'Was Eddie *Bryce's* baby?'

I held my breath, not even picking Alice up on her sheer bluntness. I knew she wasn't usually that rude. She was just trying to raise the topic as quickly as she could, and make the question as clear as possible to that poor, addled brain.

Lucy looked so confused. I wasn't sure if she'd been rattled by Alice's ruthless tone, or didn't know the answer. But suddenly I was *exasperated* with this pathetic woman who had let that great bully ruin my son's life. So I pitched in as well. 'Lucy, *is* Bryce Harris Eddie's real father? Or was there someone else before him?'

She lowered her head, trying to duck the question. Her hair fell over her face. But I was fired up enough to say to her sharply, 'Lucy!' and it worked a treat. The tears leaked and she panicked, whispering, 'Bryce said never to tell.'

I thought, if bullying *works* . . . 'Why *not*?'

I barely caught a word of what she mumbled next. '. . . nobody's business . . . couldn't prove it . . . not stop his money when he left . . .'

('*When* he left', you will notice. Not even '*if*'.)

174

'Why? Had that happened to him before with other girl-friends – that people had gone after him for child support?'

Her head was almost on her chest. I had to lean in even closer to hear. '. . . got so *angry* . . . had to keep moving . . .'

I left it there, and by the time Eddie came back, Alice had soothed and charmed poor Lucy back to smiles and nods. But when the three of us were on our way back to the car, I drew ahead with Alice. 'Well done for starting that. At least we know.'

She turned to check that Edward was still out of earshot. 'So, will we tell him?'

'Only if he asks.'

She kicked the gravel up in little sprays. 'He won't, though, will he? Poor Eddie's totally *allergic* to any questions about himself. Asking *or* answering.'

And do you know, till Alice said that, I had never realized.

Clarrie Tennant, Year Group and English Teacher

We had high hopes of him. He was so bright. When he moved to us from his primary school he was amenable and willing. Studious, even. Like several of the others, Edward used work to hide the fact that he found socializing quite a strain. He was quite often to be found up in the library. And in the lunch hour, he would disappear for half an hour or so to get his homework done somewhere in school.

He was a pleasure to teach. You had to press him hard to make him speak up willingly in class discussions. But you could rarely fault the stuff he wrote, except in trivial ways. He had a very wide vocabulary for his age. And he was thoughtful.

Then, that term, he closed down – and it was pretty well overnight. It was the strangest thing. All of them go through changes. From time to time, the girls get in some weird moods. Tearful. Aggressive. Mardy. You have to cut them quite a lot of slack. We are quite used to that.

The boys change too. It helps to learn to ignore a lot of the sullenness, and not pick up on all the petty rudeness. It's not an easy time. Some lad who never gave a thought to what he looks like suddenly comes out in spots. His face erupts, and it's as if his personality implodes to match. He hides his head, won't raise his hand in class, he misses clubs he's always liked, and can't scoot off the premises quickly enough after the buzzer sounds. The ones that haven't started on their growth spurt become self-conscious as the others tower over them or flaunt themselves in the showers.

Then there are those who just lose interest in the work. They sprawl across the desks, and you can almost see them counting off the minutes till they can leave and, as they put it, 'get a proper life'. You have to keep on trying to kick-start them into a bit of effort, and stamp on all the tiresome waves of bad behaviour born of sheer boredom.

Sometimes you want to shake them all till their teeth rattle.

All normal. All in a day's work.

But that term Edward was quite strange. It was as if his wits had wandered off. He wasn't rude. He didn't seem unsettled. How can I put it? More as if he *wasn't there.* As if some alien craft had landed overnight to sweep off the real Edward and leave us with this dead facsimile who just went through the motions. If I am honest, he reminded me of my grandmother after Grandpa died. She smiled and nodded and she did her best, but her heart wasn't in it. She was half-drowned in echoes and reminders: 'Your grandpa loved that song.' 'That would have made my Eric chuckle.' 'Oh, how he *hated* beans.' Whenever I visited, I felt as if there was another person in the room, far more alive and real than me.

Edward had gone a bit like that — as if he was beset with shadows.

We asked his parents in, of course. That's standard. They're a perfectly nice and sensible pair. Mrs Stead made a point of reminding us that Edward had a difficult start in life (though she admitted he had seemed to triumph over that). Her husband sat there with a worried look. 'I'll try to talk to him,' he kept on saying. 'I *have* tried, but I'll try again.'

What can you do? We had to leave it at that.

Then, pretty well as promptly as it had begun, the phase was over. Edward was himself again.

Eddie

I'd had a vile day. Mrs Tennant on at me about not listening in class. Nicholas watching me with that stupid worried look. Natasha nagging me about mess in the kitchen, and Alice screeching on about something I'd said in school that had got back to one of her best friends and caused a row.

I stomped out of the house, telling them that I needed to fetch some homework that I'd lent to Justin. I wasn't bothered where I went, but I just had this passing thought that Nicholas might take it in his head to follow me. So I walked down to Justin's street, and saw that elder brother of his hanging about in front of the line of garage doors on Lenby Lane.

That's when I thought of it. It wasn't before.

When I told Troy what I wanted, he looked me up and down as if I were some sort of plonker. 'Blueys? I ain't had any of them since longer than *for ever*.'

My disappointment must have shown. 'Tell you what, though. I've got these.' He dipped in his pocket. 'Just as good. Some reckon better. Want a go?'

'How much?'

He took me for a total ride that first time (though I smartened up and never paid so much again). But that night all that mattered was that I had it in my hand – a passport to what everyone wants. That sense of peace and warmth and calm. (Everyone in the world believes in peace. Believers pray for it. Newsreaders go on about the chance of it in practically every bulletin. I'd even heard Natasha mention it when her phone rang at night. 'Oh, no! The only thing it seems you can't have in this world is peace and quiet!')

The quiet bit was easy. Nobody, not even Alice, bothered me once I'd announced that I was off to bed. And peace came stealing in almost as soon as I had taken them, those lovely little red pills. I did feel guilty, of course. But I could defend myself. After all, hadn't Alice pretty well *insisted* I was a druggie?

So why not prove her right?

Those were some special evenings that I had, all by myself, sprawled like a starfish on the floor, safe from all thoughts of Harris. And all the good stuff lasted through the day, because a thin leftover thread of calm did seem to make it easier for me to look as if I might be trying at school. It helped at home as well. Knowing that I could soon be off in my own cradled, timeless universe made it far easier to bat away Natasha's questions without a loss of temper. 'Edward, what were you doing in the bathroom for so long last night? I reckon you were there for *hours*.'

I wasn't going to say a raging thirst had sent me for a simple glass of water but, twisting off the tap, I'd seen the first drip gathering, silvered by moonlight, and taking a lifetime to swell in perfect beauty. I'd watched entranced as the slim shining rim of it along the tap edge tirelessly budded till, quivering, it broke away to drop onto the porcelain with such a rich and echoing chime I had to make an effort to remind myself it would not wake them in the other rooms. Regretfully, I'd watched the little tadpole of the drip slip down the plughole. And yet already, on the tap rim, another was gathering – fat, gleaming, mesmerizing.

Had I stood there all *night*?

I loved those pills. Natasha caught me on the landing once, staring down through the banisters at the rug in the hall. She didn't know that it was swirling in obedient patterns. In my own head, I could make all its colours twist and turn, not clumsily like in a kaleidoscope, but with a buttery smoothness, as if the myriad shades of red and orange and ochre were merely following my will.

'Edward?' She smiled. 'What are you up to? You look miles away.'

'Just thinking.'

'What about?'

'Nothing.' But even I could tell that sounded wrong. 'Well, actually, something a little complicated to do with homework.'

She ran her hand over the top of my head as she went

by. 'I am so pleased with you. And so is Mrs Tennant. I was just coming up to tell you that she rang today to say you're doing *so* much better.'

And I was. Somehow the things my brain and I were doing together at night made everyone around look different. Once, after I'd ill-advisedly jumped the pill-popping gun, I was called back downstairs because of one of Rob's rare evening visits. And it was magical. I realized that, under the skin of everyone round me, I could still see the creature they had been in childhood – just as, when I was taking my first bluey, I'd once seen Alice. I knew, just knew, that Nicholas had been unmercifully teased about his hand when he was young. Watching him join us in the living room, I saw how he unthinkingly made for the chair which best hid his bad hand, and I ran through my head the recent times I'd seen him take a seat.

At the pub picnic table.

In the dentist's waiting room.

Down at the railway station.

Always the same, I realized. Always the chair that kept his left arm turned away as if it were a horribly scarred secret. Why did he still do that? None of us ever teased. Natasha even shared his bed. Why would it be a habit, if he'd not learned to automatically protect himself so much in childhood? I'd watch Natasha, and see her as the strained and anxious child she must have been when she was sent away at ten years old, so eager to stay friends with everyone in boarding school that she could not relax, no, not even now, all these years later in her own home. I must have been much easier to live with in those months, while I was seeing both of them the way I did, as vulnerable children who had put on some toughened shell of grown-up habits. They were much happier now that I seemed less anxious in their company.

I even started asking them all sorts of questions.

'Natasha, do you get much time to read at boarding school?'

I wonder if she thought I wanted to leave home. 'It isn't easy, Edward. Everywhere you are, people are always there.'

'But you can surely slip away and read?'

'There's not much slipping away.' She puffed her cheeks out childishly, as if simply remembering had sent her back in time. 'And every time people in my school left a book somewhere, either it vanished or some grim teacher made a scene.'

'A scene? About a book? In a *school*?'

'Oh, not about your reading it. About it *being* there. You know.' She launched into an imitation of some fusspot teacher. '"Whose is this book, Marie? Who left this on the windowsill? Hermione, is it yours? Have you just left it lying about for someone else to pick up? No? Then, Clarissa! Was it *you* who left it here?"'

'It sounds quite horrible.'

'I'm sure that things are far, far better now. But back in my day you were kept so busy that the only time you had to read was in the dorm before lights out.' She scowled. 'And even then somebody else had probably borrowed your hair.'

'Borrowed your *hair*?'

'To practise plaiting. So it was hard to keep your eyes steady on the words.' She smiled at me. 'I'd never have been able to even *try* to read that smelly book with tiny print that you're forever stuck in.'

'*The Devil Ruled the Roost*?'

'It would have been impossible to even *start*.'

'Except in holidays.'

She gave a hollow laugh. And I had heard enough about the way Natasha's school breaks had turned into running battles between her warring parents and their second families, to guess that escaping into books had not been easy then. Alice had confidently claimed that was the reason why Natasha wanted us – so she could have a second stab at living in a peaceful family.

So maybe I can't blame her for never noticing my drifting ways, my times of quite unnatural reverie, the hours I spent locked away.

Or all the money vanishing from her purse and Nicholas's wallet. 'Don't trouble Trouble till he troubles you,' she always said. And after all, I was no longer wandering around the house at night. I slept much better and was worrying less. All that I had to do to calm

183

myself was count the hours till I heard one or another of the family come out with what I had begun to equate with buzzers signalling the end of the school day. 'I'm really bushed. I think I'm turning in now.' Sometimes I did catch Alice watching with a quizzical look. But she was busy now – falling in love with boy after boy in headlong fashion, all of them somehow staying friends and rushing off whenever possible in some merry, ever-changing group that Nicholas began to call 'Alice's flock'.

Alice

He only ever dared to steal from me once. He slid a single note out of the money clip I kept in my desk drawer. I suppose he hoped I hadn't counted it.

Well, he was out of luck.

I went downstairs to Nicholas's office and took a couple of squares of plain white card. I cut out arrows – twenty-five of them. Then I went into Eddie's room and took down one of the photos that Natasha had framed of Eddie looking thoughtful in the garden.

I hung a mirror on the hook instead.

I laid down arrows in a trail across the floor from the door, then stuck a few more running up the wall, to reach the mirror.

Above the mirror I stuck another arrow, pointing

down. I wrote in tiny print, so he would have to go up close to read it:

Face of a thief.

Not only did it work, it shook him up so much that he said sorry. It was quite obvious that he'd been crying.

I felt so *mean* – using a mirror to torment poor Eddie with his own face. I know that I cried too. And then the two of us made up.

Eddie

That summer, Justin's brother lost his usual source. 'Try these instead.'

'No thanks. I'll stick with the reds.'

Troy scowled. 'You'll have to find them somewhere else. I've not got any more.'

Weakly I took the twist of paper he was offering me. 'Same price?'

'You're lucky, Eddie. Even cheaper, these.'

But I threw most of them away. I tried them only twice. Both times the dreams I had were vivid. Terrifying. Worse, they were *unforgettable*. I'd rather have had Harris haunting me than those vile crawling things that made their stinking home inside my brain. I swear that I could actually *smell* them.

They wouldn't go, not even when I forced myself to stay awake till morning.

'God, Edward! You look *terrible*! You're *trembling*, even. What on earth's the matter?'

Natasha took my wrist. 'My Christ, your pulse is *racing*. And you're *thick* with sweat. Quick, back to bed at once.'

No thanks! Another vigil like the one I'd barely left behind? Those vicious voices with their grisly whispered threats? That feeling in my lungs that every bodily cell was being squeezed by devils, starving me of air, and I was going to choke? No, thanks!

'Honestly, I'll be fine.'

'I'll call the doctor.'

'No!'

And I was lucky. Natasha was in a hurry to leave for work. She left a note for Nicholas, who was already in his office, still in his dressing gown but busy on a call – something to do with vandalism overnight at one of his sites. The moment Natasha left the house with Alice, I snatched up the note. *N – call surgery for E. Tell them important.* She'd underlined that last word twice. I crumpled it into my pocket, and dropped on the sofa. Linda's slow breathing trick took time to work. But it was a long phone call, and by the time that Nicholas came through to make his coffee, I had left the house.

Everyone knew where to get those bright cans with even brighter names. Just half a mile away there was a shop run by a half-blind, worried-looking Sri Lankan woman. The secret was to count your coins, take off the tell-tale school jacket and stuff it out of sight inside your bag. You went into the shop and hung about till she was busy with another customer. Then you snatched up the cans you wanted and rushed across to dump your money on the counter just in front of her. You'd flash the stolen proof-of-age card in her face and use your gruffest voice to mutter, 'That money is exactly right. Sorry, here comes my bus,' as you were hurrying out.

I'd done it! I had bought the card from Cerys months ago, mostly for form's sake, just like everybody else. But up until I made it around the corner, safe, I'd never truly thought that anyone in my school year could get away with it.

And yet I had. I doubled back along the alley, then over to the park, to the old bandstand. Slipping beneath the pock-marked *Keep Out* barrier, I picked my way up the five rotting steps.

And I was lucky. There were no tramps in there sleeping it off. No other truants hiding from nosy adults. I settled back against the mildewed panelling and drew my legs in tight to keep them out of sight of anyone strolling by.

Three silver cans, each claiming more than two units of alcohol, four hundred calories, a load of grams of sugar, citric acid, sodium saccharin and God knows what else. I slugged them back in no time, proud to have thought of such a sensible way to calm my racing pulse and frayed nerves. There'd be no more red pills. Or blueys. No more

187

pills at all. No. I was done with drugs that made my thoughts no longer mine, my nights a living terror, my dreams so painfully vivid that splinters of them had the strength to haunt me over and over, even in company, even in daylight.

I sat there for a good half-hour or so. And then I scrambled to my feet, brushed the damp grime off my grey trousers and I went to school.

That's how it started – cheerfully enough. I was so busy telling myself how smart I was to pack in downing all Troy's offerings, I never thought to look ahead. I felt much safer with drink. I found it warming. It took the edge off worries, and I could concentrate enough in school. (Everyone was dead pleased that I passed my exams so well and was accepted into first year sixth.) I even found it easier to make friends – and not just with the boys who used their elder brothers' proof-of-age cards to buy alcohol that they'd sell on to me.

With girls as well.

Alice began reporting back. 'Melissa says her sister fancies you.'

'The one in Mr Goldman's class? With the fair hair? *Really?*'

'Yes, I was astonished too.'

I gave her an affectionate punch. 'Seriously, though? *Does* she?'

'She told Melissa that she thinks you're sweet.'

'*Sweet?*'

'Yes.' Alice grinned. 'She doesn't know you very well, does she? I told Melissa I'd be more than happy to point out your many flaws.'

'Thanks, Alice!'

But she and I were getting on better and better. Whenever Alice wasn't busy with the flock, she worked hard. She had set her sights on university, and since two of her subjects were the hardest ones – physics and maths – her homework often took her hours.

That's why she had begun to skip coming along on visits to my mother.

To start with, I cashed in on this, making excuses when Nicholas raised the topic. 'Alice says that she's pushed for time. We thought we'd make it next weekend instead.'

'You said that last week. And the week before.'

I shrugged. 'Oh, well. Lucy won't notice.'

'Edward, there's more than one reason to visit a vulnerable person. One of the things that keeps care workers up to scratch is knowing that their clients have people who come often enough to notice if there's something wrong.'

Now I was getting ratty. 'You're telling me it's my job to look after *her?* She didn't look after me! And now I'm old enough, I don't have to go at all.'

'All that I'm saying is that you should give the matter some thought before you just stop going.'

'I *told* you. Alice and I will go *next* week.'

★　★　★

And yet we didn't. Not that week, nor the week after. The Sunday after that, Nicholas pulled the old trick. 'Edward, I'm visiting a site quite near to Lucy's place this afternoon. I thought of dropping in. It's up to you whether you come or not. But I'll be leaving here straight after lunch.'

'This is the *last time*,' I remember muttering to myself as I got in the car. It seemed too childish to sulk the way I usually did when I felt people were pushing me around. But I was smarting.

'What do you want to do?' asked Nicholas, dropping all pretence of wanting to see Lucy himself. 'Come to the site with me, then call in together afterwards? Or be dropped off and picked up?'

'Dropped off and picked up.'

Nicholas tried to console me. 'Good plan. We'll get home quicker that way.' He didn't know that I had no intention of going in. I'd tucked a book into the bag beside the cake he'd taken from the freezer, and I intended to find some quiet place to sit and read until I saw his car draw up again.

'About an hour, then?' were Nicholas's last words.

I nodded, making a show of setting off unwillingly up the short driveway. I waited till he'd driven off, then slipped across the lawn into the narrow shrubbery and round to the garden at the back. There was a clump of laurels behind the table where the residents ate on

190

warmer days. That's where I went. I knew the sun wouldn't reach me, but I could stay reading in there until I had to head back to the gate. And I'd be out of the breeze.

Better than going inside and having to meet them all.

Except they suddenly came out. I heard the back door scrape, and then their voices as they trooped across the lawn. One of the minders must have been herding them because, before I could sneak off, the first two or three had taken seats around the wooden table. There was a bit of fussing till someone who was claiming that he was 'allergic' got a place out of the sun, and someone else had swapped her wobbly chair for something better.

But then they started on some sort of lesson. Or maybe it was therapy. How should I know? All I could hear was each of them being encouraged to sing some song they knew, some song that brought back happy memories.

I'm used to Nicholas's music pounding through the house for hours on end, so I just blocked my ears. Each time I turned a page I caught a snatch of song or conversation. One of the men had a deep, rasping voice, and sang a sad soft ballad I actually knew and liked about someone going away with no word of farewell. But most of the songs and the singers were rubbish, and I kept reading.

Then, even as I had my fingers pressed in place, something got through.

The first I realized was that I had somehow, without

even noticing, shifted myself into a sitting position and was rocking back and forth. The print that I was reading had blurred to nothing. I felt very strange.

I took my fingers out of my ears. For just a moment I didn't recognize the tune. Then came the chorus.

'Happy days, and happy ways
I hope you know how glad I am
To see you here with me today
We're going to have great fun.'

My mother's voice. Thin, reedy and uncertain. Not how she used to sing it along with me and Mr Perkins.

But still, her voice.

'That's *lovely*,' said the minder. 'That's *very* cheerful. Is there any more?'

There was, of course. Already it was ringing in my head, the verse about *making, not breaking*, and *sharing a dream*. But clearly that was long gone from my mother's brain because, almost at once, someone else muscled in. 'If Lucy's finished, then it's *my* turn now.'

I don't remember any more. I know I forced myself back through the laurels till I reached the fence, then worked my way around. I left the cake at the side door and hurried to the street.

When Nicholas showed up, he was appalled. 'What on earth's happened to you? You look all red and lumpy!'

I shrugged. 'Just nettle stings.'

'Nettle stings. On your face? But *how?*' He peered at me more closely. 'Edward? Have you been *crying?*'

There wasn't any point denying it. I'd barely stopped.

'Oh, Christ!' He pulled me in the car. 'God, I am sorry! We've been brutes, pushing you into this. But if this is the way it's going to get you, maybe you're right. It's time to take a break from seeing Lucy.'

I started crying again, of course, when he said that. I was in such a mess. I didn't want to see my mother. But I did. The thing is that I didn't want to see my mother like *that.* All stupid. Not my mother. Not even able to sing a simple song she'd heard a million times. My *favourite* song for years. (Pretty well the only one I knew back in those days, of course, but that was not the point.) I didn't want to come and spend a boring, hateful hour with this dumb Lucy who was nothing to do with me because the punch bag Harris made of her was not my mother.

What I wanted was my *mum.* My *first* mum, who had known the song, the *whole* song, and who sang it *properly.*

They couldn't do a thing with me. I cried for hours. I think that Nicholas even tried to get in touch with Rob at one point, but there was no reply. He'd been retired for months in any case. And what would he have known? In the end, I so wanted them to go away, I forced myself to stop my sobbing and pretend I'd fallen asleep. Natasha slid a fresh, dry pillow under my head, and once she'd sat for a while, trying to make sure that I wasn't faking, she finally went back to Nicholas, who'd taken the first shift then gone to bed.

As soon as I was sure that they were both asleep, I crept downstairs.

Gin doesn't only come in silver cans, as something bright and fizzy. You can slug it back from bottles too. I've no idea how much I drank that night. I know I had a good few inches, mixed with orange from the fridge. And then I poured some more into a mug and took that back upstairs. I drank the lot — so much I was surprised I wasn't sick as well as dizzy.

Then I fell asleep.

That's how it started getting out of hand.

Alice

I blame myself. I should have realized. You see, I'm not like Eddie. I can take or leave it. I got in with that crowd. Some of them dropped tabs. Some of them drank a bit. A few did both. And quite a lot did neither.

I had a lot of fun. It never occurred to me that I was giving Eddie something that would steer him off the path the way it did. I had no problem myself. I spent a few months acting a bit wild, and then I saw that telly programme. There was that girl in her third year of university and I just wanted to be her.

I started working. That was that. I still went out some nights, but I knew what I wanted more than getting wasted, and I made a space for it.

People like Eddie – well, they're not like that.

Eddie

The thing is, you don't notice. It happens gradually, the fact that so much of your energy is going into getting drink, then trying to disguise from everyone the fact you've drunk it. There is Natasha, telling you about some major accident she's driven past, with blue lights flashing, helicopters overhead and police cars all over. Only a few weeks ago, you would have been agog, keen to hear every detail, ghoulish questions pouring out of you. 'Did you see any *bodies*?' 'Do you think that anyone was *dead*?'

Now you're just nodding away and trying to look interested. But all your real attention is on her purse at the end of the table. How much is in it? How long since she took the money out of the machine? Is it safe to assume that she's lost track by now, and if she digs in there to pay the window cleaner or to buy some aspirin, she won't be puzzled to find herself more short of cash than she thought. Maybe start counting back. Let's see. Twenty to Sarah for that extra cleaning. Another forty spent on photographic paper. Alice's lunch money. But where's the rest? I know I took three hundred out only two days ago.

Where has it gone?

I had to take great care. It took a deal of effort to recall how many notes I'd slid out yesterday and the day before. By then, of course, I'd found far cheaper ways of buying stuff. There was this really ropey shop down by the railway station. You'd walk around a bit to check that all the deadbeats hanging about outside smelled really bad or reeked of alcohol. (The rest were said to be narks.) Then you would sidle in. I'd settled on a brand that was, quite literally, as cheap as chips, with some ferocious-sounding Russian name I never really mastered. (I only had to point.)

And you'd be sorted for the next couple of days.

I usually mixed the stuff with orange. Either Natasha's freshly squeezed juice or, if there was none left, cheap orange fizz. Arif traded that. He nicked it from the back store at his mum's corner shop, and he'd take anything in return: some old CDs, a couple of sleazy magazines, a bottle of spray perfume Alice had sniffed at once and then chucked in her bin. He even took a ballpoint off me once. 'It's a bit chewed at the end. Does it still work? You're not getting much for that!'

The first to notice was the dentist. 'Four fillings, Edward? All out of nowhere. Have you stopped brushing? Or have you started eating sweets all day?'

I don't know what possessed me. I thought I'd try to do my teeth a favour and learn to drink the stuff neat.

It wasn't half as hard as you'd imagine. Within a week or so I had begun to enjoy the brutal wash of spirit against my gums, the way it stung the tiny cracks in my lips.

I never overdid it. I was determined I would not become one of those drunks Natasha so despised, who end up vomiting all over everywhere. So I learned never to go over the top, just let the alcohol ease off the tiresome edges of the day. I think it helped that I wasn't in a gang, so had no problem when I'd had enough. It was my bottle. I could screw on the top and put it back in its hiding place whenever I wanted, even if there was some left. I think it's different if you're out with friends. Perhaps your mates don't even ask before they slam another glass of what you're drinking down in front of you.

Alice could go for days, probably weeks, without even thinking of alcohol. But when the flock were out to celebrate the end of exams, or someone's birthday, things were quite different. I'd seen her staggering about, presumably after one of the gang who was already in an oiled-up mood had come up with the bright idea of getting one or two more cans or bottles of whatever it was that they'd been sharing. Mostly she made it safely up to her bedroom, after first putting on a pretty impressive show to Nicholas and Natasha. 'No, I'm not tipsy. I had one glass of wine at Sarah's, and even then Safira drank most of it. Oh, yes – and then I had a few sips of Jason's beer. But I'm not tipsy.'

A fine performance.

She would pretend to take a brief interest in the news bulletin that they were watching, then yawn a couple of times, and make it to the bottom of the stairs without once swaying. But she would grip the banisters as she came up, and pass me with a conspiratorial wink. Then there'd be phone calls. After that, I'd hear her clean her teeth and run a shower. By then, Nicholas and Natasha were often upstairs as well. But only I would notice the soft click of Alice's door as, only a few minutes later, she padded hastily along the landing to lock herself in our shared bathroom. It was what she would call 'the swirling pits' – a giddy feeling of nausea that took her over the moment she lay down and closed her eyes, making her realize she'd drunk far too much and felt so awful that she wanted to die.

'Why don't you stop before you reach that stage?' I'd ask her, perfectly sincerely. 'Why carry on and have the one that shoves you over the edge?'

She'd shrug. She didn't really know. She always regretted it. She vowed she'd be more sensible next time. And never was.

But Alice only went out now and then. Once a month, maybe?

I thought myself so much more clever with my own 'little and often' habit. Oh, sometimes things panned out so I lost track. Something at school annoyed me, or I got too wrapped up in music I was listening to, and didn't notice how many times I'd tipped a little of the magic stuff into the plastic beaker that I kept around me. But I was only rumbled once, and that was by Natasha, who fancied that she had an eye for boozers. 'Edward, have you been *drinking*?'

I'd only just that minute brushed my teeth, so I affected outrage. 'No, I have not! What makes you think that?'

Her eyes narrowed. 'It's the way you're standing there.'

'*How* am I standing?'

'Just a bit too steadily.'

'That is because I have two feet, and I've been practising for fifteen years.'

She couldn't help but laugh. 'Don't you get smart with me. There's something odd about the way you're stand-ing. And you have that look.'

'What look?'

'That really still and careful look. As if you have to calculate before you move. You're standing like a jug that's worried that it's way too full and thinks it might slosh over.'

'A worried jug? Now who is sounding like the one who's had a few?'

She had to chuckle again. But it was still a warning shot across the bows. And when I checked the cabinet the following day, sure enough she had drawn the tiniest little pencil mark across each bottle's label at the level at which the contents stood. I knew she would have counted the beers as well.

And possibly the money in her purse.

So I nicked something else: a bucket and some washing-up liquid. Telling them I had promised to help paint the back cloth for the next school play, I cycled off to clean cars in a supermarket car park on the other side of town. I didn't do a brilliant job, and wasn't paid much. But it was enough to keep me going until Natasha's worry died away, and she had been distracted again by work.

It more than once occurred to me that I could go down to the garages and try whatever it was that Troy was pushing now. It would be cheaper, certainly. No doubt about that.

But then I'd catch myself shuddering. I'd no desire to take that risk again. I felt as nervous about it as when you wake with a start from some appalling dream, swamped with relief that no, you're not being chased into a pit of snakes, or holding a grey and greasy baby with snapping teeth. You know you're safe, but still it takes a bit of time for terror to fade. You even force yourself to stay awake an extra minute or two, in case it's true what all those primitive tribes believe – that the dream world is real, and all that nightmarish stuff is truly happening somewhere, and if you let yourself go back to sleep too fast, you might end up back in the same fix again.

No. That pop-a-pill-and-send-your-brain-all-haywire stuff was not for me, and I'd stopped dead on it. So I knew I had willpower. Why, I had even earned my racing bike as a reward for stopping gnawing at my nails. The drinking was a *choice*.

At first. And then, of course, it practically became a hobby. And then a sort of obsession. I'm telling this, of course, from way, way on. If you had said to me back then that alcohol was taking over my life, I would have snapped your head off. But it was true. I always had the next little top-up in mind. I started keeping bottles in useful places: one on the way to school, hidden behind a rotten strut in the bandstand. One in the cistern of what I had come to think of as my personal lavatory. One under the garden shed, so I could have a swig before I went back in the house.

I think I thought of them as little staging posts along the day.

And I stopped going to things – even things I wanted to do. 'You're coming on our picnic?' Melissa's sister asked. She was already blushing, so I knew what was in her mind.

It was in my mind too. I'd really taken a shine to Rose, and thought about her a lot. But still I hedged. 'Picnic?'

'For end of term. We're going to Harts Park, and just before it closes, we're going to hide so we can swim in the river.'

The people at Harts Park might not be brilliant at counting people out at night, but they are good at checking bags on the way in. It is an alcohol-free zone.

'Not sure,' was all I'd say.

'Oh, come on, Eddie. It'll be *fun*.'

I knew it would be fun. Especially in her company. But not for me, because I also knew I would be thinking only of when I could get back to take a slug or two from one of my bottles. Already I'd begun to feel quite tense and itchy when I was away from all my little stores. I wouldn't yet admit that I was hooked. But I did know what I'd begun to think of as my 'time limits', as if it was a reasonable thing for someone my age to act like one of those alkies down by the canal who would go crawling after anyone, desperately begging for 'just a couple of quid, just for a sandwich' when everyone who passed them knew what they would spend it on.

I think my problem was that I'd spent so much time praising myself for being far too smart to get addicted to Troy's drugs that I'd not realized that the other stuff had taken such a grip.

And, when I say 'the other stuff', I do mean anything that had a kick. The preference for clean, pure vodka was long gone. I would drink anything now. Every few days, when Nicholas was busy and Natasha was out, I tiptoed into their room and squeezed a line of their toothpaste out into a little pot. That way I could still clean my teeth a dozen times a day but not have to add another Mintgleam tube onto the shopping list each week, or pay for one myself. I learned to quite like sherry. I learned to quite like cider. In fact, I learned to quite like anything that had the right effect.

Except for beer. I wouldn't go near that. Even the smell of it reminded me of Harris, and made me nervous. Since I had seen his face in mine, I couldn't even walk past beery-smelling pubs without it coming painfully to mind that he was my blood family.

And then, of course, I'd need another drink.

I am astonished that I kept my secret so long. Mind you, I was cunning. 'How did you get that bruise?' someone would ask, and even before I had inspected the vivid purple mottling I hadn't even known was there, out came the answer, glib as anything. 'Tripped on some stupid wire.'

'What are you up to?' one of the teachers asked when she caught me in one of the cloakrooms during lesson time, rooting through pockets. 'Forgot my antibiotics,' I answered, quick as a flash.

It couldn't last, of course. I started being late for school, or bunking off early. Often I didn't go at all. I did a lot of sneaking about by then, no longer confident that I could get past Natasha's watchful eye. During the rush of breakfast, I'd casually set the scene for my delayed return, talking about an extra football practice, or bragging about being asked to supervise junior detention. But still, when I came home, I'd watch the shadows on the window blinds till I was sure Natasha had moved into the living room, or Nicholas was in his study on a call.

That's when I'd slip in the house and hope to make it up the stairs before they challenged me.

Then things got worse, and I became more careless. Right at the start, I had been cautious with the empty bottles. I'd wrap them up and smuggle them out of the house. I would make sure I was at least three streets away before I tipped them into some recycling box left by a gate. And, just in case, I'd never use the same box twice.

Then I stopped bothering. It all seemed too much effort. Now I would tip the bottles into the first recycling tub I saw on the way from our house to the bandstand. One day a householder rushed out as I was throwing back his lid. He was a tubby, gentle-looking fellow, a bit like Rob Reed. 'I wouldn't mind,' he said. 'And it sounds really petty of me to say it. I ought to thank you for not littering the streets or leaving broken glass lying about. But, you see, I'm a minister.'

I hadn't had the wits to take to my heels. So I just stared.

'Methodist,' he explained. 'I am supposed to be tee-total. That means I never drink.' He smiled. 'So it's a bit embarrassing to have your parents' bottles shoved into my recycling each week, alongside my blameless jam jars.' He dug in his pocket. 'Here, tell your mum and dad I've written down the council number, and if they phone they'll get a bin of their own. They're all delivered free.'

'All right. I'll tell them.'

'Have a good day at school.'

I'm sure that I lost track and used his bin again. But by then I was losing track of lots of things, not just how much I drank but sometimes even where I'd been. I'd reach into my pocket and find odd things. I opened up the side flap of my backpack once to see two twenty-pound notes, and I had no idea where I had stolen them. Sometimes at weekends I would lose whole hours, suddenly realizing that I had no memory at all of what had happened between leaving the bandstand and sneaking back in the house.

The drinking showed as well, not just in my poor schoolwork and ratty temper, but in other ways. I found that I was sweating all the time. My ears buzzed. My eyes twitched. I found that I was picking quarrels and insulting girls. I itched and scratched. 'Stop *doing* that!' Marina said one day when we were paired for biology.

'Stop doing what?'

'That scratching. Stop it! Stop it *now*!'

I couldn't, though. I had to leave the room.

And all the time I was still congratulating myself for my self-discipline and my good sense. *I'm not like that*, I thought each time I passed some drunk in a doorway. I started fussing about the oddest things. Once, I remember handing back a sandwich Arif didn't want because the meat in it was 'stuffed with additives'. Me, who was *hungry*, and had been pouring poisonous and brain-deadening liquids down my poor throat for months!

Till Alice finally laid down her pen after her last exam and looked around her properly for the first time in weeks.

I heard the back door slam. 'Natasha! Nicholas!'

But, rarely as it happened, neither was there. I heard her charging up the stairs and threw myself against my door to bar her way.

Too late. She burst into my room, punching the air with both fists. 'Finished! All done! I'm free again! Don't even care if I have passed or failed! At least it's over!'

She didn't even wait to hear my mumbles of congratulation. We were so close to one another that she sniffed. 'What's that weird smell?' And then she peered at me. 'Eddie, you look like *shit*! What is the *matter* with you?'

I don't doubt I responded sourly, 'Nothing.'

Her nose was wrinkling again. 'It's you. You actually *smell*.'

'I don't.'

'You do. You'd better have a shower before you come out.'

'Out?'

'We're going to *celebrate*. At Valentine House.' She saw my puzzled look. 'You know! The end of my *exams*. You must remember! Nicholas reminded you this *morning*.' Now she was studying me even more closely. 'What's *wrong* with you? Why are you acting funny?'

'I am not.'

'You are.' She dived towards the bed cover. I lurched to stop her but I lost my balance and fell, hard, on the floor. By the time I had pulled myself into a seated position, Alice was back on her feet again, holding the half-empty bottle.

'You cunning old soak!'

I tried to make light of it. 'Oh, come on, Alice. Everyone has a drink now and again.'

She studied the label. '*Volkogonova?* Forty-two per cent proof! Well, that explains why Nicholas and Natasha aren't even back yet!'

She was losing me. 'Not back from where?'

'Didn't they tell you? Back from your school, where they've been called in to discuss the fact that you skipped half of your mid-terms and failed the rest.'

That should have made me stop and think. But all I wanted was for her to give me back my precious bottle and leave me alone.

Natasha

I hadn't noticed, you see. For one thing, it was our busiest time of year. All those June weddings. Malcolm and I were trying to decide whether to keep on renting extra marquees or take the plunge and borrow to expand the business.

And Edward had been so much *easier* those last few

weeks. Much more relaxed. Now and again he'd even followed me around the house, asking about my own childhood. (His foster mother Linda had told me he did that with her, and I remember being disappointed after he came to us that he seemed rather too shy to ask me questions. I worried that I might not seem the motherly type to him. But in my job I have to look smart and professional at all times. There's no way round that.)

Nicholas too had just assumed that things were fine again. He was astonished when the phone call came to ask us to come in a second time.

I will admit that I was irritated at the thought of yet another meeting. It seemed to me that Edward was doing better all round. He was no trouble at home. He claimed that he was keeping up at school. He went to bed at reasonable hours. What was their worry?

I reckon half the staff must have been there. I was appalled at what they told us. It was a catalogue of sins. Copying other people's work (or not even bothering). Failing his mid-term exams. Telling a host of lies. Bunking off school.

Drinking.

That came as such a surprise that Nicholas didn't even grasp what they were saying. 'What do you mean, drinking? Do you mean mucking about with water bottles in class?'

'No,' Mrs Miller told us. 'Drinking alcohol. In school.'

We sat in silence, both of us, all the way home.

Edward

It was a God almighty bollocking. Of course they tried to be reasonable at first: calm looks, soft voices, gentle questioning. (Those therapy sessions with Alice when she went through her rebellious phase had clearly left their mark.) But as my inability to answer properly – or, as Natasha termed it, 'stubborn refusal to even *try* to explain' – began to rattle them, Natasha's voice became more loud and hectoring, till Nicholas was spending almost as much time trying to calm her down as he was getting at me.

And he *was* getting at me. Alice claimed afterwards that they were especially angry because one of the staff implied that people with adopted children lacked the insight of natural parents. (She'd heard Natasha spitting tintacks about that the following day, threatening to write a letter.)

But I think they were furious because they hadn't guessed. Now it was pretty obvious to both of them that they'd been blind. The moment they came through the door, Natasha called me down and Nicholas brushed past without a single word as I came in the kitchen.

Natasha kept her back turned, fiddling with the kettle lid while I stood waiting, not sure what to expect.

Then Nicholas came down, swinging three bottles from the fingers of his good hand: two empties from my backpack because I'd been too careless to get rid of them, and the one Alice had pounced on under the bed.

'Edward? Do you think you could very kindly explain the presence of these bottles?'

It all came out. I was berated for falling behind in practically all of my subjects, lying to everyone and bunking off. But mostly for the drinking. It seems the janitor had seen me stumbling in the corridor and watched me going in the private lavatory. I stayed in there so long he worried that I might have fainted. Then, through the door, he heard the soft clink of the cistern lid.

After I'd gone, he'd found my bottle and told Mrs Miller.

Brilliant.

Natasha's cheeks were burning. 'Edward, where did the *money* come from?'

I wasn't going to *hang* myself. 'I cleaned cars. Ask them at Merryfield. I'm in their car park a lot. I wash the cars while people go into the shop. I don't charge much, but most of the women tip me.'

'I don't believe I'm hearing this!'

I turned on Nicholas. '*You* drink! You have a couple of gin and tonics pretty well every day.'

'I'm not at school! I'm not fifteen and taking my exams! And I'm not telling lies and probably stealing things to get the money.'

I don't know where I could have got the sheer self-righteousness to hurl at him, 'Is that what you *think* of me? That I'm a *thief*? That's nice! That's trusting!'

He rolled his eyes. 'Why should we trust you? That's what all this is about! You *can't* be trusted. Not here, and not at school, and probably, for all I know, nowhere at all!'

'Well, thanks!'

It was Natasha's turn to lose her temper. 'Don't you get uppity with us! It's you who's been behaving like a guttersnipe!'

We all froze then. Alice. Me. Nicholas. Even Natasha herself. She knew what she had said. I think we all were thinking of where I'd come from.

All of us had Harris in our minds.

She tried to cover her tracks. 'Edward, all that I meant is that the people in a family have to be confident that no one's keeping secrets behind their backs.'

Nicholas pitched in to help. 'Look, this has been a really testing evening. I think we're all worked up. What I'm suggesting is that we all calm down—'

'And have a *drink*?' I asked sarcastically.

He flushed, then just pushed on as if I hadn't spoken. 'And we can try and talk about it all again, without getting upset, once we've had supper.'

I don't blame Alice for coming out with it. It didn't help, but still I think she had a right to say it.

'Too late. We must have lost our table ages ago.'

'Table?' And then Natasha remembered. 'Oh, God, Alice! I'm so sorry! Today was your last exam!'

'It doesn't matter,' she said.

But we all knew the efforts Alice had made over the

211

last months not to throw down her stupid test papers and slide off with the flock whenever they rang up. The *hours* she'd put in. The extra work she'd done. We'd all seen the revision chart she'd made and hung up on her wall, over her desk.

We all knew she'd been sitting there counting the days. I bet they both felt terrible.

But I felt worse.

Louise Smith, Manager of Valentine House

You come across some tiresome people when you run a restaurant. The Stead booking was down for seven o'clock. No one had come by twenty to eight. And then a group of four called by my desk on the off-chance.

'No hope of dinner, I suppose?'

'Give me a moment,' I said, and rang the contact number for the empty table. It was a woman who answered.

'*Yes?*'

She snapped as irritably as if I had deliberately interrupted her while she was adding figures.

I told her, 'This is Valentine House.'

'Oh, God!' she said. 'Oh, *God*! Well, I'm afraid to say that we're not coming.'

If she had just said sorry I wouldn't have told Rosalie

to charge their credit card our No-Show fee. (It is quite steep. We only have one sitting.) And I did have four people staring at me hopefully. The restaurant would not be out of pocket.

But all she said was, 'You wouldn't want to have the four of us in any case.' She raised her voice, presumably for the benefit of someone at her end. 'Because one of our party is *a bloody liar* and a *drunk!*'

I held the phone a little further from my ear.

'Thank you,' was all I said to her. 'Have a good evening.'

Then I turned to the waiting group. 'Your table's ready. Please will you come this way?'

Eddie

I had a rotten night. Maybe it was from missing my night-time beakerful. Maybe it was just guilt. By morning, though, my only feelings were resentment and bitterness. Natasha had been very rude to me, and Nicholas was treating me like a child. 'I'll drop you off at school today, if you don't mind.'

'Thanks, but I'd rather walk.'

He didn't even try to soften the insult. 'No, Edward. After what we heard last night about your attendance record this term, I think I'd rather make sure that you actually get there.'

So it was pretty well a challenge, really. And I was

certainly feeling grumpy enough to take him up on it. I reached the gates, and fell in step with Tina and Martin, who were taking turns to tug at Justin's scarf. I went inside with them, and then peeled off. As soon as the buzzer for registration sounded, I rushed past the monitors by the front door – 'Forgot to lock my bike!' – and left the school.

I crept around the far side of the hedge to find my bottles. One was stashed down a tree stump and the other one was pushed behind some crates stacked for the Friday pick-up.

There wasn't much in either. But fortified by that, and by self-pity, I wondered what to do next. I don't know why it sprang to mind to go to see Linda and Alan. Their house was over sixty miles away. I didn't even know if they'd be in. But once the idea surfaced, I was determined to go. I didn't think of it as 'running away' as such, though obviously after the meeting the day before, someone at school was bound to ring Natasha and Nicholas about my absence.

And I would be away for hours, getting to Beasley and back.

Still, off I went, stuffing my school jacket way down in my bag, and walking to the western roundabout where I'd seen people hitching often enough before. I think the white shirt helped because I got my first lift almost at once, along with a lecture about the dangers of hitch-hiking. 'Surely you're old enough to know that half the drivers on the road are maniacs, and the rest fools. I tell you, if you were *my* son, you'd be in really big trouble for doing something so stupid.'

I grinned. 'Is that the only reason you picked me up? To give me a ticking off?'

'Yes,' he said sourly. 'And I would hope that someone else would do the same if my lad Larry acted as daft as you.'

That killed the conversation dead. But he did leave me in a sensible place for my next ride. That was a lorry driver who could barely string two English words together. He had an accent rather like Stefania's. 'Are you Romanian?' I asked politely. You would have thought I'd asked if he were an axe murderer. God knows what nationality he was, but he went on and on about it really irritably. I didn't understand a word.

But once again I was dropped somewhere good, and it was only another couple of short rides before I found myself crossing the park in which I'd learned to work my way up on the swings so many years ago.

They were both in. 'Eddie! What a surprise! Come in! Come in!' Already Linda had noticed that I was in uniform. 'Taking a day off school?'

'I couldn't face it,' I admitted.

I watched her take care not to miss a beat. 'It's *ages* since we've seen you. Light years! You've grown so *tall*! Come in the kitchen and tell us all about everything!

What do you fancy, sweetie? Tea? Coffee? Juice?'

I didn't feel like anything except a proper drink. But there was no chance of that so I said, 'Tea, please,' simply from politeness, and sat at the table eating their chocolate biscuits and telling them about Natasha and Nicholas, answering questions about my subjects at school, and how well Alice was doing.

'She got held back a year. But now that she's switched subjects, everything's fine and she's made up her mind to go to university.'

'And what about your mum?'

'Lucy?' I shrugged. 'I still see her a bit. She's much the same.' Into the silence that followed, I added, 'But she is happy. She likes the place she's in a lot.'

'And what about *you*?'

The nitty-gritty question. What about me?

If only lying weren't so downright *easy*. I had a choice, clearly. I could have let it all pour out, about the drinking. After all, they must have known that something was wrong. Why else would I turn up there unannounced like that, nervously rattling my tea mug, fingernails gnawed to the quick again, looking like death? It's not as if I didn't give myself time to think what to say, because that was the moment I picked to ask to go upstairs. (The bathroom seemed horrifically bright. I had got used to Natasha's stylish lighting systems. And on the way down, I opened the door to my old room. It was much smaller than I remembered it, and looked more dingy.)

After they'd bullied me into eating one or two cheese sandwiches, we moved to the living room. I suppose they thought it would be more relaxing – make it easier for me to tell them what was going on. But I just bottled out. 'Everything's fine,' I kept saying. 'I simply woke up feeling really rough, and couldn't face the idea of being in school. So I bunked off and hitched down here, just on the off-chance.'

'Life's batting on all right, though?'

'Pretty well. I mean, I get fed up at times. But mostly things are fine.'

I'm sure they realized I was hiding something. But still they let it go. I suppose they didn't have much choice. After another half an hour or so, Alan looked at his watch. 'Righty-ho, Ed. If you plan to be back when they expect you, then it's time to get you moving.'

I knew he'd give me a ride home. I could see Linda was very tempted to come along. But I think she decided in the end that Alan would have a better chance of getting something out of me if he and I were travelling alone.

Down at the garden gate she gave me an enormous hug, and then she told me something.

'You know that television man of yours? That Mr Perkins? Well, Alan went online and found one of his programmes. Just out of curiosity, you understand.' She found my hand and squeezed it. 'Because we missed you.'

I couldn't help but ask. 'What did you think?'

She smiled. 'I loved it. He was very sweet and fatherly. I wish they'd showed the programmes here, not just in Canada. They would have been a hit. The songs too. Though I must admit they do stick in the brain and drive you mad.' She started singing the one about growing up to do anything we wanted.

> *'Some things seem very hard to do*
> *You think you won't be able*
> *To get them right,*
> *But then you do*
> *And you win through—'*

To pass the last sticky moments while Alan was bringing round the car, I prompted her when she got stuck.

> *'Because you're strong and brave inside.'*

We finished it together.

> *'But most of all, of course, because you want to,*
> *Want to, want to*
> *Because you're strong and brave inside*
> *And really, really want to.'*

Linda

You just can't tell with people Eddie's age. What's for the best?

If he'd been four, or eight, or even twelve, I wouldn't have given it a thought. The moment Alan drove off with him, I would have snatched up the phone. 'Natasha? Nicholas? I ought to tell you Eddie bunked off school and came to us. And he seemed rather upset. Rattled. Distracted. Horribly unhappy. He couldn't sit still and barely smiled. Is something wrong?'

But teenagers are so *mercurial*. One minute they act forty, the next minute *three*. You can't judge much from a short visit and, for all we knew, the boy was being truthful when he said it was the first time he'd played truant. It was a year of constant, stressful school exams. And he had always chewed his nails until they bled.

I paced around the phone for quite a while, wondering what to do. I even phoned Rob Reed's old number, but it didn't work. (I didn't fancy ringing any of the new lot. Eddie had been adopted now for years, and they would just have given me one of their lectures about 'letting go'.)

So in the end I told myself not to betray his trust. And I tried to console myself that, if he was in trouble, my darling, darling Eddie would have the confidence and the good sense just to come back to us.

Eddie

Alan got me home in time – well, only a little late. And no one at the school had rung to tell them that I wasn't there. I got away with it.

I suppose I could have taken the chance to settle down and start afresh, but I got irritated by the way they treated me that week. Nicholas did as good a job as any Gestapo officer of searching my room. He found the bottle tucked away under the shed. And when the restaurant at Valentine House charged his card that hefty whack for our No-Show, he made it clear I wouldn't get a penny of my allowance until I'd paid him back.

Natasha was worse, though. Clearly humiliated by the way I'd got away with so much for so long, she started checking on me about everything.

'You *did* go swimming, didn't you? I mean, your shorts are damp, but they don't smell of chlorine.'

'How come you've got no homework? Mrs Miller made it crystal-clear that this is a crucial year.'

'Nicholas told me that he drove past your school at half past three, but didn't see you.'

I'd fight back. 'Probably because there are about *four hundred* of us pouring out of there. We're all in the same uniform, and he might just have kept one eye on the road.'

She took against my tone. 'No, Mister Clever Dick. He'd parked right by the gates. He said that he was hoping to give you a lift.'

I told her sullenly, 'He must have been at least half an hour early, waiting to pounce, if he found anywhere to park near the school gates.'

She made me feel as childish as I must have sounded. I hated being watched. She studied me as if I were some specimen in a jar. She'd swung from over-credulous to ludicrously suspicious. It was quite obvious she didn't believe a word I said. She was so *hostile*. Even Alice thought that, and she herself had given me a good few days of the curled lip and cold response.

But in the end she started sticking up for me. 'Leave him alone, Natasha! He's grounded. Isn't that enough? There's no need to be picking on him all the time. He's said he's sorry.'

Actually, I hadn't. I'd hung my head, and I'd admitted things, and I had claimed that I'd turn over a new leaf. But I had never said that I was sorry.

I wasn't, either. I was in a sweat, missing the constant swigging that took the edge off things. I went to school all that next week, and realized, in my stone-cold sober state, how far behind I'd fallen and how much I had to do to catch up with the rest – even some of the thickies.

Even Justin.

That hurt. The only thing that ever gave me any confidence was hearing people saying I was bright and did so well at schoolwork. Now that prop had been snatched away. And it seemed so unfair because the rest of them were hardly angels. I'd hear them in the cloakroom, bragging about how many tinnies they had downed last night, how off their faces they'd been, how they'd been 'smashed' or 'mortal'. I couldn't understand how they could binge like that, and come in looking pale as grubs and acting ratty and dull, but then next day, like Alice, they'd be bright as buttons again and concentrating on the work as if the mere idea of this stuff being in the world had faded from their minds.

I couldn't be like that. I thought about it all the time. How I was missing it, how I could lay my hands on some. When Jessica invited me back to her house along with Arif and Trish to see her brand-new puppy, I made an excuse at first. (I always made excuses.) Then I remember thinking, *Perhaps her family has a drinks cabinet.* I actually *thought* that. In break, I pounced upon a couple of grubby plastic bags blowing around the bike shed, so I'd be ready.

And then I tagged along. Jessica didn't ask what made me change my mind. And while the three of them were letting the frenetic little fur ball tumble all over their feet and Trish was shrieking at the sharpness of its teeth, I slid away, reckoning that I could claim that I thought any door I might have been caught opening led to a lavatory.

I was in luck. They kept their bottles on a pantry shelf. I lifted off two full ones at the back. Vodka and gin. I stowed them in my school bag and left it lying by the door. Then I went back.

'You found it?' Jessica asked.

For one heart-stopping moment, I wondered if she meant their stash of spirits rather than their loo. But still I managed to nod.

'Good. Sometimes there's trouble with the flush.'

'I didn't notice.'

'You were lucky, then.'

And off the conversation went, on to the usual stuff about the times the girls had found themselves staring at something that wouldn't flush away, and how embarrassing it was. Arif pitched in with some disgusting story about a coat hanger and a giant turd, and they were giggling and pushing him. 'Shut *up*, Arif! Shut up!'

'I have to go,' I said. 'You know I'm grounded still. If I'm not back by four fifteen, Natasha will go wild.'

'Poor Eddie! Just for getting sozzled *once*.'

Is that what I had told them? I must have lied to *everyone*. I still faked coughing fits and went round the cloakrooms, pocketing anything that I could find to trade for booze money. I watched myself with Nicholas and Natasha because I knew that they were watching me, and even leaving money about to test me. Once or twice I even nicked a pound or two from Valentina, sneaking the purse out of her bag while she was busy cleaning. (She soon stopped leaving that about.) Now and again I dragged my plastic bucket out from where I stashed it, under next door's hedge, and started washing cars again – until in desperation one day I sold my bike, pretending to Natasha and Nicholas that it had been stolen.

'Really? Where had you left it, Edward?'

'Down at the river. I was with Arif. But I had locked it, and we were only a short way away. If anyone had cut the chain, I would have heard.'

'You're telling us that someone came along, lifted it up and carried it away silently on their shoulders?'

I gave them one of my almighty scowls. 'All that I'm saying is, it's *gone.*'

There followed one of those great pauses designed to remind me that I was no longer trusted. And then Natasha said, 'We don't see anything of Arif these days, do we? I mean, you *talk* about him quite a bit. But he no longer comes this way home with you, or calls by to pick you up.'

It was quite clear what she meant: 'I don't believe a word you say about being with Arif. We think you use his name to hide what you are really doing.'

Oh, they weren't daft. But still, they couldn't watch me every minute of the day, or keep me grounded for ever. And sometimes I had money. Each time I had enough, I'd lay my hands on yet another bottle. But now I wouldn't take the risk of hiding them about. I'd work my way through them in one fast session.

The rows we had got more and more frequent, and very much nastier. 'We will not have you coming in this house in this disgusting state! Look at you! You can barely stand!'

'Leave me alone! It's *my* life!'

'Not while you live under our roof! How you behave is our business too!'

'Oh, back off, both of you! Leave me *alone!*'

And, pushing past them, I would stagger to the stairs and drag myself up to my room. Sometimes I'd rushed the drinking so much I was sick. Once I lashed out at Nicholas, and he nearly punched me back. Another time, after we had been screaming at one another about some sin of mine, Natasha lost it utterly and screamed, 'Oh, Jesus Christ! I wish to God—'

She broke off before saying it. But we both heard it ringing round the room. 'I wish to God we'd never adopted you!' It was another reminder that I came from bad stock. That my blood family were foul and nasty ne'er-do-wells.

Right then, I'd think, I might as well not worry. Being like this is pretty well in my stars. And Nicholas and Natasha can't boss me around for ever. Soon I'll be old enough to do what I please. I found my ears were pricking up when, in maths lessons, Mrs Pugh gave people who were mucking about her regular ticking off: 'You won't always *have* to be here, you know. A good number of the people in this class are almost old enough to get a job out there in the big world, sweeping hair cuttings off the floor or stacking supermarket shelves. So if you're not willing to *apply* yourselves . . .'

It suddenly sounded very real. And relevant. Not that much longer and I'd reach the magic age.

I could leave school.

And home.

There wasn't simply one last straw. It was a host of things, all piled on one another. In one short morning I did worse than Justin in three tests in a row. That was a shock. I think I'd thought that, just by turning up at school and sitting through it, my work would soon bounce back. I came home in the foulest mood and found a note from Nicholas on the kitchen table: *Eddie, back from site at six. Please smarten up for going out for supper.*

That's all I need, I thought. An evening out. The two of them asking me endlessly about my day in school with Alice sitting all relaxed because she'd finished all the exams that mattered.

I heard Natasha's car door slam. Knowing that if I could make it to my room I wouldn't have to go through all the questioning twice, I made for the stairs, getting there as the door opened.

Speeding up, I stumbled on Alice's school bag.

I kicked it. Hard. Before it even skidded off across the parquet floor, I'd heard the tell-tale sound of something breaking.

Alice spun round from where she'd been standing in the kitchen doorway, talking to someone on the phone. 'Eddie, you *pig*! You've gone and smashed my present from Melissa!'

Of course. The reason we were going out. First I

forget the day she finishes her last exam. Then I forget her birthday. And she'd stuck up for me so many times. She made excuses for me. She'd been *brilliant*.

Guilt makes you fight back harder than you should. 'Your fault! You shouldn't have left it in the way like that.'

Alice was outraged. 'You bloody *booted* it! I *saw* you. You're a little shit!'

Natasha was in the house now. 'Alice! You watch your language!'

Alice spun round. 'It's Edward's fault! He keeps behaving like an *animal*!' She turned to look me in the eye. 'Acting as if he has some *beast* inside him!'

Oh, didn't Alice know how to boot back! That word 'beast'. So well-chosen.

Fine! I remember thinking. *You brought Bryce Harris into this, so I will act like him.*

I lifted up my foot and smirked at her, and then I brought it down – *crunch* – on the rest of what was in her bag.

Alice turned white with rage. 'You nasty, nasty little piece of work! You creepy shit! Why don't you piss off out of this house, and go back where you belong! Nobody wants you here. You're spoiling everything for everyone. And we all *hate* you.'

Natasha stepped in. 'Alice! You take that back at once!'

She wouldn't. She was burning up with fury. 'No! No, I won't! You two won't say so, but it's *true*. He's ruining this house with all his sulks and tempers. He leaves revolting messes in the lavatory when he throws up. I don't know how poor Valentina stands it. He's crap at school. He's got no friends. He tells lies all the time. Justin's mates say he even steals from people's bags and pockets. He certainly lifts things from shops! He's rude and vile and horrible and *smelly*.'

I didn't think she knew all that. I was dead shaken. But I expect I slapped on some infuriating smile. I know I said, 'Excuse me. I am off to take a shower – since I'm so *smelly*.'

Alice burst into tears, and I ran up the stairs, away from the whole boiling mess.

I waited. But Natasha never came. I couldn't believe that. After all those things that Alice said! Each minute that passed, I felt more like a worm.

I was quite sure Natasha would come up to talk to me. I knew that she'd be absolutely furious. (It can't be nice to learn that someone in your family is known outside for a thief.) But Alice had announced that the whole house would be better off without me.

Worse. That they *hated* me.

Surely Natasha would come up and say it wasn't true.

But then I heard her going into Alice's room. That really riled me. Yes, it was Alice's birthday. But, so what? I'd never even *tasted* birthday cake till I was eight years old. Alice was eighteen! You'd think she could have managed to get over one cracked present by herself. I knew if I'd said half so many vile things about her in all those months when she was being such a pain, nobody would have come into *my* room to comfort me first. Nobody would have rushed to sympathize with *me* about some stupid ruined birthday gift.

But then it struck me that, although Natasha had been sharp with her – 'Alice! You take that back!' – she hadn't said it wasn't *true*.

Maybe it was.

I waited. But she never came.

Alice

I felt so *awful*. I was the only one who knew how much the idea of Bryce Harris haunted him. Nicholas and Natasha knew about the face Stefania showed him on her computer screen. But only I knew the idea of being like his father was driving Eddie mad. (If you have been adopted, you don't go on too much about your thoughts and worries to do with your 'real' parents. It seems ungrateful and rude.)

So I let Eddie down. I'd actually *seen* the look of horror on his face after he stamped on the bag. He might as well have howled, 'Oh, please God! Don't let me have done that! That is what *Harris* would have done!' So only

I knew how much I had rubbed it in when I used that word, 'beast'.

I should have simply rushed across and thrown my arms round him. 'It doesn't *matter*, Eddie! It's just *stuff*.'

But I was angry with him. I said all those things . . .

Oh, I felt *awful*. And then he wouldn't let me in his room, and I felt *worse*.

Eddie

I left that night.

Nicholas banged on the bedroom door when he came home, but I refused to answer. I was busy packing.

I thought it through. A couple of T-shirts. Jacket. Spare socks and pants. My thickest woollies. Knife. Torch. You would have thought that I was off on a school camping trip, not planning to go away for ever from where I wasn't wanted.

While Nicholas and Natasha were talking in the living room – no doubt about my sins – I went into their closet to snaffle the money belt Nicholas had worn all through our holiday in Italy (even though, when he left his watch on the beach, at least four people had called after him, and one great tub of lard had actually prised himself up from his towel to chase us and hand it over).

I was barely back before Alice rushed up the stairs and

started banging on my door. 'Edward! Oh, come on, Eddie! Let me in.'

I didn't answer. She kept knocking for a while, then went back down to report. I didn't pack much else. Everything useful, like my birth certificate, was locked in Nicholas's safe. But I did want to make the point that I was never coming back, so I took most of the Mr Perkins tapes out of my old Life Story Box and jammed them into the backpack, along with my copy of *The Devil Ruled the Roost*.

I sat on my bed and waited. Nicholas came upstairs and tried my door once or twice. 'I'm leaving you some supper here outside.' And, 'Edward, it's getting late. I think perhaps we'd better talk about all this tomorrow morning.'

An hour after they had shut their door, I pulled the supper in and scoffed the lot. Then I crept down to steal some raisins and chocolate from the kitchen cupboard.

There on the bottom shelf I saw Natasha's purse. She'd clearly shoved it in there in a hurry, once the fuss started. I must have rooted through more thoroughly than usual because, in a side pocket that I'd never noticed before, I found a faded scrap of paper. *I owe Patricia Ness £39.72.*

Who'd write a note about a silly amount like that? No one. You would write £40, even if it were true. And I had never heard Natasha mention any Patricia.

Patricia Ness? Pin Number.

Bingo!

I took the bank and credit cards, picked up my back-pack and slid out of the house. I was in luck. The pin worked on three of the cards. I walked away from the machine with such thick wads of notes I had to spread them all round the money belt.

I didn't want to let myself be tempted into trying any of the cards again. I knew, if I did that, they almost certainly wouldn't work and I would have to think of Natasha phoning up the bank and either admitting to them that her own son was a rotten thief, or telling them some lie in hopes that I'd come back and pick up life again.

I didn't want to have to imagine either. I snapped the cards in pieces and tossed them in the nearest skip.

And then I left.

IV

Natasha

When Alice shouted all that stuff at Edward, my heart turned over. I felt as if a thunderclap was ringing in my ears. I couldn't *think*.

Was it because I felt that way myself? Or feared I did? Lord, what a question!

It's always possible. I had been doubtful about adopting, yes. Who wouldn't be? I'd always wanted to have a family, but can't pretend I didn't think that they'd be really mine – by blood, I mean. I wasn't into doing good by other people's children. But Nicholas had been quite *devastated* by the words the doctor said: 'No chance at all. I'm sorry.'

I sometimes wondered if, left to myself, I wouldn't have simply cried myself to sleep for a few weeks, and then gone back to building up the business. But, though he tried to hide it valiantly, and comfort me, I couldn't help but notice that Nicholas had gone all quiet, as if some plug had been pulled out of his life plan. You should have heard the music that he played continually through those first weeks. 'Music to cut your throat by', I'd have called it, if I hadn't been trying so hard to pretend I hadn't noticed, just to keep poor Nicholas from feeling even worse.

And then, I felt so *guilty*. I know! I know! But inasmuch as there is any meaning to the word in things like this, it was my 'fault' in that it was my body, not his, that had let us down. And neither of us had a clue when we got married. We had agreed we'd have a family, and that was that.

Nicholas wasn't the sort to hear the bad news and say, 'Sorry, Natasha, but I can't imagine a life without my own children. So I'm off.'

Which left me stuck.

And then I saw the corner of that booklet tucked away between some of his sheaths of plans. He'd either picked it off the rack at the Health Centre or sent away for it. It didn't matter. I felt obliged to ask, 'Nicholas, have you been thinking about adoption?'

And we were off.

I couldn't spoil our chances in the interviews by being *totally* honest. I must have said all the right things. I do remember it was understood by Nicholas and myself that he would do the lion's share. And he did too. He never grumbled (though in a quarrel once he did say that he got the feeling I'd rather be outside the house earning the money to pay for things for the children than take them with me to the shops to actually buy them).

Mostly, things worked out fine. Nicholas had what he had wanted most, and so did I. I found both children far, far easier to love than I had feared – first out of pity, of course; but then from something so much stronger.

I'd make the very same decision again.

Yes. Yes, I would.

Eddie

I look back now and reckon that if I hadn't hitched to visit Linda and Alan only that short time before, then I might not have run so far away. I might have simply gone to them. I would have told them about Alice rubbing my nose in it, reminding me I was blood family to the Beast. They would have understood. They would have phoned Natasha and Nicholas, suggesting I took a few days to calm down again. They might have even put me straight about the drinking. Things might have come out right.

But I felt, stupidly, that I'd tried that. I thought I'd look pathetic – babyish – if I went back so soon.

This time, I thought, I had to shift for myself.

So I went north. That was pure accident because, when I looked at the station departure board, I saw the first train going out was heading off that way. I wasn't daft. I bought a ticket only as far as the next town. Then I got off and, after switching jackets in a lavatory cubicle and pulling on a woollen hat I'd nicked from a bike basket,

I went to the machine there and bought another ticket, heading somewhere else.

In the next place, I took the hat off but pulled up my hood, and tagged behind a gang of boys my age, all buying tickets to somewhere called Cold Ash Halt. I bought one too, hoping that anyone scanning security camera images afterwards, in search of me, would simply think that I was one of their group.

Cold Ash is where I spent the night, curled with my vodka and sandwiches in a back doorway at the end of a deserted side street. I'd had so much to drink I had to count Natasha's money several times before I got the same result twice in a row. I knew I was quite safe, spreading the notes in front of me in separate piles, over and over. The place was such a one-eyed hole they had no cameras about. If I'd stayed long enough, I probably would have seen the locals pointing excitedly at aeroplanes. But first thing next morning, after dumping a few of the Mr Perkins tapes into a litter bin to make room for more bottles, I was back to the station and away.

To the first major city.

Manchester.

Things are so strange in big cities. I hadn't realized. Most of the people on the streets walk past as if you were invisible. Then somebody turns up acting as if the two of you have been best friends for years.

That's how I met Barry, mooching about in front of a

vegetable stall. As I walked past, he stuck out an arm to stop me.

'Hey!' he said. 'What's that weird purple thing?'

I looked at where he was pointing. 'That? That's an aubergine,' and added, only because I knew, 'Some people call it an eggplant.'

He snorted. '*Egg*plant? Why would you call it an *egg*plant? It's nothing like an egg!'

He had weird bulgy eyes and the most clumsy way of walking I'd ever seen. But somehow we just fell in step.

'What's in the backpack?' he asked.

'Just stuff.'

'Clothes and things? Why, are you going to your dad's?'

I hid the bolt of shock and just said, 'Sorry?'

'You know,' he said. 'Fed up with Mum. Going to Dad's to get as fed up there?'

I caught on. 'Is that how things are for you?'

He shrugged. 'Not any more. Now I just stay at Mum's and I don't bother with the other house. Dad's Mandy is a *witch*.' We reached the corner. 'I go up this way,' he said. 'Why don't you come along?'

He saw my anxious look. 'Come *on*,' he urged. 'Come meet my mum. She will be glad to know a real professor.'

'What?'

He grinned. 'You know. Whatever you said about those purple things. Auber – auber—' He gave up trying to remember. 'Eggplants! Mum likes it when I bring home clever mates.'

★ ★ ★

I'm sure if I'd picked up some stranger three years older on the street and brought him home, Natasha would have raised one very frosty eyebrow. Barry's mum was different. For one thing, she was unbelievably young, with slinky, sexy clothes and bright dyed hair. Her name was Jaz (short for Jasmine) and I thought that she must have left school and had Barry when she was only about *twelve* until he told me she was thirty-six.

Still, I was on my best behaviour that first day, and when Jaz realized I had nowhere else to go, she let me stay. 'Just for tonight, mind.' But Barry had been right when he said that his mother wanted him to bring home mates. She clearly worried about him being the sort of boy who found it hard to make friends. (They'd called people like Barry 'dafties' in my school, and they were all the same. Too keen. Too willing. Sort of *desperate*.)

And Barry wasn't very bright. He said the same old silly things over and over, till you stopped listening. I think his mum was bored in any case. She was 'between jobs'. My arrival made some sort of change. She offered straight away to put my grubby stuff into her washing machine, and asked all sorts of questions. (I told all sorts of lies.) She even sent Barry off next door to borrow their camp bed so I could stay the next night.

And the next.

I think Jaz had me down as 'interesting'. First, from the

way I spoke – all 'booky', as she put it. And secondly because I seemed to her to know a lot. Over the next couple of days I helped her fill in the form to get back Barry's child benefit which had been going to his dad. I helped Barry with his homework. (It was so simple that I realized he must be in a special class.) I even knew enough from all the hours I spent helping Alan in the shed to show Jaz how to sort her window box.

Both of them thought that I was wonderful. Almost exotic. A rare animal. Even the way I vanished all the time when Barry was at school interested Jaz. 'What do you do all day?'

I'd shrug. 'I wander around the city. Look at things.'

In fact, I drank. I'd very quickly fallen back into my old leave-the-exact-right-change-and-rush-from-the-shop technique. I'd offer Barry the occasional swig. He'd shake his head, 'No, thanks,' and reach out for the bottle of sweet orange fizz I'd bought for him while I was pick-ing up my rip-off Russian vodka. 'Your stuff just hurts to drink.'

I introduced my bottles to the house. (It was a risk, but the alternative was long dry evenings.) Jaz took a sip or two now and again, but only after drowning it in Coke. And once or twice she ticked me off when we were watching telly. 'Go steady, Ed. That's half a bottle already.'

The days passed. Talk of when I would move on just

seemed to die away. I paid my way with food. And since what they liked eating was the cheap stuff – bread, pies and pizzas, with the odd take-out curry for a treat – the money that I'd stuffed into the money belt saw me through day after day. I think that Barry thought I was producing bank notes magically. But Jaz was on my case. 'Where does it *come* from, Eddie, all that money?'

'I earned it. I washed cars every weekend and saved the lot.'

She didn't miss the chance to put in her pennyworth. 'Then you're a fool to dribble through the whole lot, pickling your brains.' It was quite obvious my charms were wearing thin. After a few more days she'd had enough of tripping over empties and finding me still slumped in one of her armchairs when she came down in the morning.

I wondered if I should go home. I *wanted* to go home. I looked around Barry's cramped and dingy bedroom and thought about the cheerful, spacious place I'd left, with its bright desk and matching shelves. The covers on the bed that Barry slept in must have been a thousand years old. The ones on the camp bed were *grey*.

I was embarrassed, though. To crawl home! To admit I couldn't cut it in the outside world.

To have to shuffle through the door and face the three of them – Natasha, Nicholas and Alice.

Cue for another swig.

Nicholas

Someone had put the music back in the wrong sleeve. I thought that I had slid in Kraftwerk.

Out of the speakers came that Roxy beat he used to love so much. I swung round. Was he just sitting there grinning? Had he come back?

What a grim mess! Natasha, swivelling between furious and worried sick. The police, initially confident – 'You'll see. He'll soon be back' – and then consoling.

And poor, poor Alice, filled with guilt.

Eddie

I reckon that I must have stayed at least three weeks at Barry's house. My being there made him so happy that, irritated as she was by all my drinking, Jaz still put up with me. I tried not to be too much of a pain. I thought of things to do. I got so bored I even cleaned the windows one day. And several times I went with Jaz to the shops to carry all the heavy stuff home in my backpack.

While I was pulling out the last few things one day, Barry began to sniff. 'What's that weird sickly smell?'

He pounced on a buckled side flap I hadn't thought to empty out before the shopping trip. 'What's this in here?'

I looked, and he was holding up *The Devil Ruled the Roost*. 'What does it look like? It's a *book*.'

'You've read it, then?'

'Of course I've read it.'

'Good, is it?'

I didn't feel like trying to explain, so I just said, 'It's brilliant. Why else would I be lumping it about?'

'Read it to me?'

I had already realized that Barry was useless with books, so the idea of reading to him didn't seem that weird. And Jaz, who had been scowling at the bottles I'd nagged her to put through the till for me, looked really pleased. So over the next few nights I read *The Devil Ruled the Roost* to him, chapter by chapter, until he'd start complaining that I was slurring my words too badly for him to follow, or reading the same page twice.

Reading it out loud made the story sound a little different. More grim. It also gave me time to think about the ways in which the boy's life started the same way as mine, and set me wondering once again about my mother.

And that gave me an idea of how I could let everyone know I was all right without sounding feeble or sorry. I bought a postcard and addressed it to Lucy at Ivy House. 'Just to let you know everything's fine,' I wrote. 'I'll see you soon. I hope you're well and happy. Sorry about not bringing cake.' (I only wrote the last bit because there was still loads of room and since I couldn't think of anything else to say, I shoved that in to fill space.)

I added, 'Love, Eddie', and stuck on a stamp. The post-card sat in my pocket for a couple of days until I found myself outside the bus station, beside a coach that said 'Leeds'. The driver had just opened the doors.

I picked out a frost-top lady who looked sensible, and just as she was clambering up the steps I thrust the post-card at her. 'Will you post this for me? It's stamped and everything.'

She pointed over my shoulder. 'See that pillar box? Why can't you post it yourself?'

'Please,' I begged. 'It will stop my mother *worrying*.'

I knew she'd understand that. I shoved the postcard at her once again, and then I fled. I was quite confident that it would be delivered. Nicholas and Natasha – and probably the police as well – would have told everyone at Lucy's home that I was missing. The message would immediately filter back that I was alive and well.

In Leeds.

And I was glad. I couldn't bear the thought of going back and facing everyone. But I had long since stopped enjoying the idea of Nicholas and Natasha lying wide awake night after night, imagining my body sprawled in some wet ditch. And from that very first train ride north, I had felt bad for Alice. For all that she'd been such a bitch with that stuff about the Beast, I didn't want her going round feeling so miserable and guilty she couldn't bear the thought of leaving Nicholas and Natasha batting around an empty house while she went away to college.

So off the postcard went. I wandered back to the estate. By then, I was bored stiff with Barry. He was such a twerp. But still, the house was cosy and it's not as if I had anywhere better lined up.

But Jaz, it seems, was getting even more fed up with me. That night I threw up on her knotted rug. Next day, she sent poor Barry off on some fool's errand, and sat me down.

'I've had enough,' she said. 'I thought you were a good lad when you came. And you were nice to my son. But now I think you're just a terrible example. I want you to stop drinking in this house. That, or you have to go.'

I suppose that was my second chance to drop the habit. (And to go home, a new boy.) But I was driven by the stuff that I was pouring into me. I didn't feel that I had any choice. I lied, of course, promising the bottle I was halfway through would be my last. But Jaz was neither as busy as Natasha nor as trustful as Nicholas. She let just one day pass, and then, while Barry and I were out, she rooted through my stuff and found my stockpile of emergency supplies.

When we got back we found her waiting in the doorway, my backpack resting against her knees.

'Go in,' she said to Barry. 'Go in now.'

He obviously knew that tone of voice. He went past like a lamb.

She rolled the backpack forward, off the step. 'Take it,'

she said. 'Everything you came with is in there. Don't come back again. And if I find out you've been lying in wait for Barry anywhere between here and his school, don't think I won't phone the police. I expect they'll wonder what you're doing mucking about with someone his age. I wouldn't try it.'

I knew what she was getting at. I stumbled off.

A warm bed and three meals a day must make a massive difference to how booze works on you. The day she threw me out I walked about for hours, around areas I had despised before, looking for somewhere I could spend the night. I wasn't brave enough to go to any cheap hotel in case my face had been on telly. So I made my way to a maze of little streets behind the bus station. I had seen alkies and dossers there – druggies my age as well – and reckoned I could follow them to find out where they slept.

It was in doorways and in empty houses – ones that the council boarded up, where somebody had broken through the chipboard to get in. Sometimes some technical whizz had even managed to tap into next door's electricity, or turn the water back on. But usually, I found out, after dark it was just candles, booze and drugs that got the people in there through the night.

I must have gone downhill astonishingly fast. All I remember is my sheer contempt for everyone round me. Look at this guy! He's turned his arms into pin cushions.

He has scabs all over. He is *disgusting*. That alky pees his pants. This new guy *stinks*. And he can hardly speak. I don't think I'd an ounce of sympathy for any of them, all driven by the crap they were injecting into their veins, or pouring down their throats. All slumped and useless and smelly.

Not like me. I might have fetched up in a grotty flat, along with a strangely shifting gang of pallid deadbeats. But I was still convinced I had my standards. I started doing quite odd things, like fretting about germs in the pot noodle tubs we used as cups. What was my *problem*? I was already pickling my liver and mashing my brain. How could I possibly have got things so out of proportion?

Was I smashed *all* the time?

Yes. Yes I was. I ran through Natasha's money faster than you'd imagine, considering the only thing I did was drink, and I drank gut-rot stuff. The very cheapest. When all the cash ran out, I took to what the others had been doing all along, trawling through supermarket end-of-day toss-outs, and finishing the half-chewed pizza slices left in the boxes people had abandoned on bins or in the gutters.

We all had ways of getting by. Shane sometimes smartened himself up enough to go round houses collecting the milk money 'early'. Mogger and Tabs went 'line shopping' – nicking things off people's washing lines that they could sell. No one who lived round there was foolish enough to leave their clothes out overnight, so you'd have thought they'd have been caught. But there was little sign of the police on the Donmar estate. Too many wild boys having wacky car races up and down the streets. Tiresome to chase and book. Unruly in the cells. And let out with a caution anyway the following morning. What on earth was the point?

Mostly we lived by what we called 'five-fingered discounts'. Shoplifting, that was. Mogger and Shane were good at staying awake all night, glued up to the eyeballs. They'd pass the time doing the stupidest things, like dropping lighted cigarettes down holes in the mattresses and bouncing up and down on them, trying to get the smoke to puff into rings, laughing like glaze-eyed hyenas.

Then, at what Shane always called 'daft o'clock', they would go out through the window, down to the Supermart on the next corner. Only one woman ever worked in there before the rest of the staff came in at eight, and she was always on the check-out. Mogger and Shane had walked out carrying heaped wire baskets sometimes, and came home with astonishing amounts of stuff.

Then Skeeter took a shine to some weird girl called Mags whose uncle ran a club. She nicked a key for long enough for Skeeter to get it copied, and after that we were away. So long as we lifted stuff in tidy cratefuls rather than single bottles, nobody seemed to notice. Mogger and Shane didn't drink. They called it 'loopy juice', and stuck to what they called 'sparking a cloud', or sniffing anything that came their way – glues and butane mostly, but I saw them getting off on varnish, petrol, weird industrial sprays and even some room freshener whose smell hung in a sickly fog above the reek of everything else.

'Why do you *do* that stuff?' Skeeter kept disapproving. (Like me, he was a drink man, though he stuck to cider.)

'More fun,' said Mogs. 'You and Ed-boy are missing out on a lot.'

So once again I had a go, and that time it was all right. In fact, it was good. I lay down on the floor and I could see up through the ceiling. Truly. I saw the whole kerbang, down to the toys on the floor of the bedroom above us. They told me afterwards that I kept jumping up to touch the ceiling to make sure it was still there. And they were laughing their heads off. Everything made us laugh. My stomach hurt from it.

Gradually I must have started coming down. That's it, I kept on thinking. And then the walls would start to swing about again, and we would laugh some more.

But there were so many times I looked around and thought, *What am I* doing? I'd glance across at Shane, curled on his grotty mattress – a sort of raft upon a sea of rags and chip papers and torn-up pizza boxes. He would be cutting himself, and crying. I'd look at the burned messes Skeeter had cratered in the pans with the result that no one else could cook. I'd see the filthy pants that Mogger peeled off in the night after an accident, and never bothered to chuck out.

I would begin to heave. I'd stagger out, shocked by the cold fresh air, to walk around and clear my head.

But all the grimness was still there. Slimy grey brickwork, so many broken windows stuffed with rags, the paintwork peeling. Every third house was boarded up, their gutters choked with weeds. The streets were thick with litter, slippery with dog mess, and sheets of metal grating covered all the shop fronts. (We called them Donmar curtains.)

Between the screech of tyres and the raw bursts of music blasting out of people's flats, there was a dismal silence all around.

Everywhere always looked *terrible*.

And so did I. I know because, when I was shoplifting one morning, I glanced up at the closed-circuit screen above the aisle, and barely recognized myself. My hair was grey with filth, my skin looked doughy and I had a wide clown's smile from massive cold sores on each side of my mouth.

I might not have believed I looked like me, but clearly someone else did. I heard a voice behind me. 'Excuse me. Are you Edward Stead?'

Six months before, I would have legged it out of there.

But I was in such a state I barely managed to shove a couple of the other customers into her path and reach the door.

She didn't chase me, but I'd seen her uniform, and once in the maze of local alleys, safe again, I gathered my wits enough to realize that my photograph must now be on some local cop-shop display. Skeeter had once explained my big mistake had been to leave home a week or so before I was sixteen. That had made me a missing minor, not a runaway, and passing sixteen after that made very little difference.

So I knew, now she'd spotted me, they would be asking around and she, or some other officer, would soon be back, shining a torch in my face as I shuffled down the street back to the communal pest-hole.

How had they known where to look?

And then the penny struck. It was the woman on the bus to Leeds. I'd been too good at picking someone sensible. She'd been so sensible, she must have written on the card to Lucy, 'Given to me to post at Manchester bus station.'

Perhaps she herself had had a son who'd been a runaway. I couldn't blame her. But even in my hopeless state, I realized that either I would be picked up and taken home, or I would have to move on.

That night, I dreamed of home, as clear as paint. I dreamed I walked to the front door and Alice opened it.

She wore that slinky green frock that Natasha bought to cheer her through her last exams.

She threw her arms round me. 'Eddie! Yeah, Eddie!' and spun round to Nicholas at the table. 'Guess who's come back!'

Nicholas was serving out some strange spaghetti shapes I'd never seen before. He looked up, smiling. 'I *knew* you wouldn't be late,' he said. 'I told Natasha.'

I woke up. I was cold and damp. I looked down at myself and cried.

Alice

I kept expecting him home. Of course I did. I couldn't believe that he could put us out of his mind like that. For weeks. Well, actually *months*. What did he think we would be thinking? I know Natasha nearly went out of her mind. She felt so guilty. 'I should have *realized*. Rob Reed did *warn* us. I should have *insisted* that Edward talked to someone.'

Nicholas practically took to drink himself. Before, he'd always stuck to one large gin and tonic in the evening. But after Eddie left, he often drank some wine as well. I'd see the bottle in the morning, neatly rinsed and put in the recycling.

I waved one at him once. 'Steady on, Nicholas, or you'll end up leaving home too.'

He blushed. And after that he got a grip. But that's a little how things were for quite a while. I felt as if I was the only one in the house who could believe that Eddie might be all right. I know that they were worried sick he might be dead.

Until that postcard came to Ivy House. The manager herself rang. I was the one who picked up the phone. She must have thought I was Natasha because she started, 'It's about your son—'

I whispered, 'Eddie?'

'The boy that's missing.'

Natasha had already snatched the phone from me. I watched the blood drain from her face. But then she said, 'A *postcard?*'

And both of us burst into tears.

Eddie

I think my brain must have turned into Stupid Soup. Instead of going home, or even waiting to be found, I pushed off further north. I'm pretty sure it was because by then with me life was a simple choice. Drinking or thinking. And I couldn't bear to think – about how frantic they must be, and how they'd tried so hard to offer me a brand-new life and I'd as good as thrown it back in their faces.

So I kept drinking. And left town. I knew from others

that the easiest train to catch without a ticket was the Football Special, running north. It was so crowded with drunks that half the time the staff stayed out of sight. I meant to leave the train at Newcastle, but I slept through and found myself tipped out in Glasgow in the early hours.

Don't ask me where the weeks went. They're a blank. I have a few clear memories. Some girl with a messy blue tattoo across her cheek dragging me into a clinic where someone bright and clean informed me that I'd let my big toe get in such a mess I could have died from septicaemia. I can remember crying when I peed my pants. I can remember stealing a blind woman's purse, and kicking the shins of some small kid who was refusing to hand over his chips.

I don't want to remember any more. All that is bad enough.

Then, finally – finally – my whole life changed.

Nicholas

I suppose hospitals don't sleep. We got the call at five minutes after midnight.

I don't believe I've ever thrown my clothes on so fast in my life.

Eddie

I doubt if I'd have been so lucky if I'd still been in the squat. I would have just been stepped around, like Charlie after he overdosed and no one realized till Stomper finally leaned over the unmoving body and muttered, 'Hey-up, mates! I reckon poor old Charlie here's been given the red card.'

But we had just been rooted out of the cellar of some leprous tenement. The other three must have been in a slightly better state than I was when the police moved us on because they were some way ahead when I collapsed in the street.

The paramedics dumped me off in A & E. I had my stomach pumped and then the nurses left me in a corridor to sleep it off, but I must still have been drunk because, checking to see if any of the bottles in my backpack had vanished during the time that I was out of things, I leaned too far over the safety bars and fell off the trolley.

It seems I made it down the corridor as far as some bright white examination room, went in and then passed out, slumped up against the door. I must have been there quite a while because the nurses had assumed I'd done a runner from the hospital while no one was watching. (Not that they would have cared. It was a Friday night. The place was humming.)

Then I came round.

Staring at me from across the room, I saw Bryce Harris. Really. We had a conversation. I remember it. 'Well, look at you!' he jeered. 'You're worse than me. At least I always managed to stay on my feet.'

'You keep away from me!'

'I wouldn't touch you with a bargepole, toe-rag! You stink! You're drunk! You're stupid!' That threatening leer that I remembered so well twisted into a grin before he added, 'And you're just like me.'

'No!'

'Oh, yes. Blood family, we are!'

Now I was weeping. 'No!'

'We are,' he told me, almost confidingly. 'You've gone right down my path. I am inside you now. Yes, toe-rag. You have the Beast living with you every day.' He licked his lips as if I were some tasty pie he was about to reach for and stuff down his throat. 'You won't be rid of me now, you little runt. Not *ever*. No.'

That's when I started to scream. That's when some burly hospital porter shoved at the door and sent me skidding over the polished tiles. That's when the nurses followed him and pulled me upright, and I saw that, facing me, was no Bryce Harris at all.

Simply a mirror.

That is what did it, I think. I didn't want to look like

him. I didn't want to be like him. And I was in a place where I could make at least one tiny choice.

I told them who I was.

I gave my real address. I told them they could phone Natasha and Nicholas. And one of the nurses told me afterwards that I asked them to lock me up so I couldn't change my mind.

They wouldn't do that, but they kept the strictest eye on me. One of the doctors wanted to throw me out. 'He's fit to go – well, as fit as he'll ever be.' But someone else did me the favour of losing my paperwork all night, over and over, so I still hadn't been discharged when Nicholas arrived.

'My Christ!' were his first words. 'What *have* you done?'

He meant 'done to yourself'. But still I couldn't help but see that child's shocked face when I reached out to snatch those chips. I swear he clung to the package out of sheer panic. If I had given the boy even a moment to think, he would have handed them over. I didn't have to raise my foot like that. And I'd forgotten that, before we phoned the cops about poor Charlie and scarpered, I'd swapped my worn-out shoes for his thick boots.

And they had studs.

Oh, God! The blood on that child's leg! It *streamed* down. But I just took off and scoffed the chips.

Now, simply remembering set me off crying again. 'Sorry,' I said to Nicholas. 'I'm sorry. Sorry about *everything*.'

'You're coming home with me?'

I held my arms out like a tiny child. 'Please, Nicholas. Oh, *please*.'

V

Eddie

It wasn't easy. But it wasn't the worst. One of the doctors at the unit told me that she thought the hardest drug to give up was plain nicotine.

After that, booze. 'And that can be dangerous, even with supervision, if you're too far down the road.' She frowned at the blood-pressure strap she'd wrapped round my arm. 'I wouldn't want to come off methadone, either, to be honest. That can be *really* nasty, and take a horribly long time.' She broke off, humming, while the stethoscope was in her ears, then added cheerfully as she peeled off the strap. 'The *easiest* one to come off has to be heroin. Almost a doddle. Cold turkey is no worse than going through a really rough bout of flu. And afterwards it's easier to keep off the habit.'

The unit cost the earth. 'Put it this way,' said Nicholas. 'We could have bought a Porsche instead.'

Natasha, for once, was gentler. 'Don't fret about it, Edward. We spent a fortune sending Alice to that school to save her going off the rails. No reason why you shouldn't cost as much, getting yourself back on them.'

I didn't see Alice for a while. The unit wouldn't let you have visitors around your own age in case they brought in drugs. It was just parents and such. They let in Linda and Alan, who brought me tons of chocolate. 'Natasha said you were *rail thin.*'

'I'm getting fatter. They make us help in the kitchen.'

'Keeping you busy, are they?'

I nodded.

Linda put on the old worried look. 'So, is it hard?'

I must have nodded again because I do remember she reached out to pat my hand. 'Alan and I, we felt so *guilty*. That day you just showed up – we knew that you were in a state. Anyone would have seen it. But we just thought it might be a one-off – you know, ploughing through exams or having some blazing row best left to cool on its own. We wondered if we ought to phone Natasha. But, you know. Meddling . . .'

I tried to comfort her. 'It doesn't matter. I wasn't ready anyway.'

She'd spent enough time around therapists to recognize the phrase. It sent her up another track. 'So, are they good here?'

I shrugged. 'Don't know. Nicholas says it costs the earth, so I suppose they are.'

'Or ought to be!' She laughed, and we went on to talk of other things. But then they realized I was getting tense and restless, so they left. I went through to the telly room to waste a couple of hours before my next session. Tiffany was alone there, picking at her multicoloured nails. The staff would never let us talk about what we'd been on. We were supposed to be 'leaving behind the person we used to be', and 'getting a new life in which drugs have no place at all. In fact, they're of zero interest'. We weren't encouraged even to guess what anyone else had been hooked on, though it was mostly obvious.

So far as I could work it out, Tiffany was the only one who'd been on the bottle like me.

'Doing all right?' I asked.

She pointed to the screen. 'It's crap. You can change over if you want.'

I cruised through some stations, then back to what she'd been watching when I came in. If we were bugged, we were bugged. Too bad. I wanted to talk.

'Tiff,' I said, 'how do you stop yourself thinking about it?'

She didn't need to ask me what I meant. 'I count to ten,' she said. 'And then I think about my primary school playground and spinning around on the witch's hat, and how I had no problem being happy back then, without it.'

'Does that work?'

'No.'

We watched some stupid bloke drive some mad vehicle over desert sands, and then she said, 'What about you?'

I wondered whether to tell her. But then I thought, *Why not?* 'I sing myself a song.'

'That's good,' she said. 'Any old song?'

'No. Always the same one.'

She reached for the remote and turned the sound off. Then she turned to me. 'Well, go on. *Sing* it.'

I wouldn't have, except she smiled – the saddest smile, as if she'd snatch at anything that might help. So off I went, through Mr Perkins's song about winning through because you're strong and brave inside, and really really want to.

'Sing it again,' she told me as soon as I finished.

'Not if you're going to laugh.'

'I'm not going to laugh.' She made a liar of herself by laughing. 'Well, obviously I am,' she said. 'But if it works, I'm going to learn it. It probably works a whole lot better than counting to ten.'

'It doesn't,' I admitted.

'I don't care. I want to learn it anyway.'

So we sang it together till she had it right. And we got louder and louder. A couple of the others came in and watched us. Tod even sang along. (It turned out he had passed his Grade 8 oboe exam and was a musical ace before he got in trouble.)

Then we linked arms and sang it as a trio in the dining room while that night's kitchen helpers wheeled in the supper:

'Some things seem very hard to do
You think you won't be able
To get them right
But then you do
And you win through
Because you're strong and brave inside.
But most of all, of course, because
You want to, want to
Because you're strong and brave inside
And really, really want to.'

The staff all cheered. (They'd have cheered anything that sounded positive.) Most of the others in the room just seemed to put up with us. They stared morosely at their cutlery. The song wasn't working for them.

I don't know if it worked for Tiff either. But she and I did sing it now and again over the next couple of weeks, and we became good friends. Tod too was much more friendly after that, and when the staff were out of earshot we swapped horror stories, and felt less alone.

Harriet Roberts, Psychotherapist

Some of these kids are really smart. (And if their parents can afford to send them here, they've probably had the best start.) We have some interesting discussions.

Take Eddie, for example. He had a hard time with 'sorry'.

'Oh, I can *say* it easily enough. And everyone is kind and acts as if the problem's smoothed over, everything's fine, we can all start afresh.' He stared at his gnawed nails. 'But that's not how things *are*, is it? I mean, there's this black patch of what you've done that sits behind you in their minds and in your own. And "sorry" can't fix that.'

'You feel it wears you down?'

'I feel I'm stuck with it.'

'Nobody's perfect,' I reminded him. 'And nor is life. It works more like a book – some pages sad, some far more cheery. And you never know what's coming next.'

'Until "The End",' he told me gloomily.

I smiled at him. 'Oh, come on, Eddie. Hopefully not too soon!'

Eddie

One morning Nicholas showed up earlier than usual. They wouldn't let me out of Group before the end, so by the time I joined him in the lounge, he had been kicking his heels for half an hour.

He came straight to the point. 'I want to tell you something. Don't say a word to Natasha if she rings, but I am whipping her off to Spain this Friday for a surprise holiday.'

Natasha hates surprises. 'You won't be popular,' I said, 'if she's got stuff to do.'

He laughed. 'I've fixed all that. I've been conspiring with the people in her office. They've filled her calendar with one or two spoof dates, and say that they can cover everything else themselves.'

'Clever.'

'Anyhow,' he said, 'it means we won't be coming for ten days. I'm sorry about that. But up till now, Natasha's been refusing to go anywhere.'

I thought I knew why that was – in case the police rang to say I was dead while she was sunning herself on some lush beach.

'I'll manage.' That sounded sour, so I made a joke of it. 'I'll borrow someone else's mum and dad.'

He gave me such a grateful smile. I realized that it had been years since I'd referred to them as 'Mum and Dad'. Alice kept using their first names after adoption, and probably feeling wary of the very word 'mum', I'd picked the habit up.

'Alice will visit,' Nicholas said. 'She's back from Bristol tomorrow.'

The place they kept us couldn't have been further in the sticks. 'She'll never get here,' I warned. 'Tod's uncle took three hours to get here on buses.'

'But Alice drives.'

That came as news. I hadn't thought what might be happening while I was gone.

'But they won't let her in without an adult. They don't trust anybody under twenty-five. It's in the thing you and Natasha signed.'

'Alice will think of something.'

Alice did. She brought my mum. She didn't spring it on me – not entirely. She rushed ahead to poke her head round the door of the room I shared with Jean-Pierre. 'Surprise coming up,' she warned. 'I did phone Linda and Alan, but Alan's on bed rest after some hernia thing, so I didn't like to ask.'

'So who—'

But Alice had already opened the door a little wider so I could see my mother wandering down the passageway, staring about as if she'd never seen a long pink wall before. Alice ushered her in and settled her on the bed till Jean-Pierre took Alice's blunt hint, prised himself out of the only comfortable chair and left the room.

'Bit of a sourpuss, that one,' Alice remarked.

'He's French,' I said.

We had a laugh about that. My mum joined in, though she had not the least idea what we were talking about. Alice went off to make some tea for all of us in the shared galley kitchen. And I was left alone with Lucy.

I thought I ought to say something, but I had no idea whether or not she even knew I'd disappeared for months on end. 'How's things with you?' I asked.

She nodded, smiling. 'We brought cake. Alice says that it's lemon.'

I had a sudden memory of Great-Granny Dinah in the home Rob took me to when I was young. She had gone on about cake. In Group, the leader had discussed the sort of damage drugs did to our brains. 'Excess of alcohol,' he'd said, 'has pretty much the same effect as being punched in the head. A boxer's brains look like the brains of an old man.'

My mother had taken punches and I'd taken drink. She'd reached the stage where she could not walk out. I'd reached the stage where I couldn't leave an inch of drink in a bottle. Apart from the fact that Lucy already had the brain of an old lady, what was the difference between us?

It was a miserable thought. But I really didn't want Alice to come back and find us sitting like two stones. So, 'Lucy,' I said, 'did anybody tell you I'd run away?'

She smiled at me. 'Eddie!'

Lord knows what that meant.

'Well, I did,' I said. 'I ran away, but now I'm back. And I'll be out of here in a few weeks. And then I'll come and see you at your place.'

She nodded brightly. 'We've been painted pink.'

I pointed. 'Pink like the corridor out there?'

She didn't know what I was talking about. But when Alice came back with the tea tray, Lucy and I were at least exchanging words. It wasn't talking really. We were just reeling off our favourite colours. Lucy had several, and I was making all mine up.

At least it was a start.

I got to talk to Alice alone while I was showing the two of them around the gardens just before they left. 'How did they take it?' I asked. 'No messing. The grim truth.'

She made a face. 'How do you think? Nicholas was destroyed and Natasha was livid. She tried to hide it, but she couldn't. You could tell that she thought they'd offered you this stable, happy family, better than anything you'd ever had, and you had chucked the whole lot in her face.'

'Ungrateful little turd, was I?'

Alice didn't argue. 'And when Natasha saw the mess that Nicholas was turning into, lying awake every night imagining your body rotting in a ditch, she said that only someone from a family as hellish as yours could be so cruel as not to even bother to ring in, even just every now and again, to tell them you were safe.'

'Not sure I *was* safe.'

'Well, you weren't, were you? When Nicholas brought you home, you looked like shit.'

'You *saw* me?'

Alice stared. 'Don't you *remember*? I drove home that very night. I was there when the doctor came to put that shot in your bum. I was there all the time that you were screaming and yelling in your sleep. I only left the next day so as not to let some college mates down in a presentation.'

I shivered. 'Glad I don't remember.'

'You're lucky. It was *horrible*. I never want to hear anyone howling like that again. Nicholas was tearing his hair out, and Natasha was striding up and down around the house all night, burning with fury and muttering to herself.'

'About my "bad blood", probably.'

'No! That's self-pitying nonsense!' Her face went tight. 'But, Eddie, since you've brought it up, there's something I did want to say. I mean, I know it was a *hateful* thing I shouted at you.' She hesitated. 'You know. About being a beast. And I've felt terrible about it ever since.' Now she was staring at the ground. 'But—'

I had to prompt her. 'But—?'

Alice looked up. 'It's not *enough*, is it? I mean, for it to be my fault, you going off like that and getting yourself in such a state you couldn't even phone home. Spending months reeling round in horrid places, halfway to *paralytic*.' Her voice was sharp. 'You're not so stupid as to think that just because your dad's a vile and stupid drunk, you have to follow his example and be one too. You even *hate* Bryce Harris! So why on earth did you *copy* him?'

My stomach clenched. And there in front of me, crystal-sharp, came a long-buried memory of Miss Bright back in primary school, leading me out of the classroom and down the corridor until we reached the tiny, safe school library with all its scarlet cushions. 'You mustn't *copy* people, Edward. I know you're sometimes not sure how to do things. But copying Astrid's painting won't make it yours. You have to take a chance and be yourself.'

Had I just nodded? Had I cried?

Now it was Alice peering in my burning face. 'Eddie?'

I shoved the ancient memory aside. 'I don't *know* why I did it. But I don't blame you and I never have.'

She darted forward to peck my cheek. (My first kiss ever from Alice.) 'Thanks, Eddie.'

Then she turned, embarrassed. 'Lucy! It's time to go!'

We walked on to the car park, my mum still trailing behind. Since it was obviously confession time, I thought I might as well be brave. 'Alice, can I ask something back? About Natasha.'

Alice looked uneasy.

I asked it anyway. 'Have I blown things for ever? Does Natasha hate me?'

'Not *hate* you, no. Of course not—' Alice broke off, to pick her next words with care. 'Though I'm not sure she'll ever truly *forgive* you.' She gave me an encouraging punch. 'But honestly, you should have seen her face when she was told you'd sent that postcard. She *must* love you, Eddie. And the two of you will come to terms.'

'She's been so nice on the visits.'

'Visits are short,' warned Alice.

'You think it will be awful after I come home?'

She shrugged. 'It's up to you. You know Natasha.

All she wants is for everything she does to be a great success. And she adopted us, so we've to be successful too.'

We'd reached the car park. Alice looked around to check on Lucy, who was dawdling behind, smiling at bushes, then she turned back to me. 'Though, to be fair to Natasha, I think that she'd be just as pleased with you if you were simply *happy*.'

I made a face. 'You reckon that's my choice? Successful or happy?'

'You could try both.' She grinned. 'That's what I'm aiming for.'

'Well, I'm not you. And I admit that, given the way I feel, I don't think happy's in the running here.'

'Well, then,' said Alice, as if this wrapped the matter up, 'you'll have to be successful. And that reminds me . . .' She tugged at the car's back door and reached inside. 'This is for you.'

She thrust a purple backpack in my arms. 'Natasha bought it. She gave poor Nicholas a helping of tongue pie for even bothering to bring your old one back when he went up to fetch you. She said it stunk the car out horribly and probably had fleas. She wouldn't even let me look inside before she dumped it in the wheelie bin. I had to sneak out later to get your treasures.'

Treasures?

All I could think of was Olly the Owl, from all those years ago. 'Treasures?'

'You know,' she said. 'The stuff you had in there when

you were carted off to hospital. I've put them in to cheer you up.' Again she grinned. 'You're going to need them too, when you see all the other stuff Natasha's put in there.'

I stood there silently while Alice herded Lucy into the car and strapped her into her seat.

A moment later, after one false start and a short spit of gravel from beneath the wheels, Alice was gone.

'The other stuff' was mostly books and papers. I did think that was odd, until I looked more closely. One of the envelopes was marked in Natasha's hand: *Edward. Fill in this form at once and post it back.*

Clipped to the papers was another clean, self-sealing envelope, already addressed and stamped.

The papers were an application for Sixth Form College, to start in just a few weeks. My good school record up till everything went wrong was all in there, along with descriptions of the courses I'd started but never finished. (The reason given for that, and for my being out of school so long, had been put down as 'health problems now resolved'.)

The only choice that had been left to me was for supporting subjects.

And that is what the books were all about. Short introductory texts on some of the options. I suppose Natasha thought that if I liked the look of one or two of them more than the others, I could choose those.

I spread the papers out over my bed and stared at them, feeling as if she'd given me a legal document and ordered me to sign my life away. She'd even used those tiny coloured peel-off strips to flag up where to date and sign.

I bet she would have forged my name for me if she had dared.

If she'd tried that on me before, I'm sure I would have baulked. Now I just didn't care. I was quite happy to have someone as tough as Natasha make my decisions for me. It stopped me having to think, and half the time I felt too muggy, the rest exhausted and tearful. Dr Ross had assured Natasha and Nicholas that once I'd stopped the tablets she'd prescribed to calm me for the first couple of weeks, I would be able to concentrate again. But I didn't bother even trying to read the books Natasha sent. I simply squinted at the jacket blurbs, then chose the ones that didn't sound too hard or dull.

Then I picked up the two things Alice had smuggled in the backpack afterwards. One was the only Mr Perkins tape that had survived. The other was the book. I couldn't play the tape, and so I read *The Devil Ruled the Roost* for what was probably the fortieth time. I knew the story so well that it didn't matter when the print began to pitch and roll, or my mind wandered off.

Until I realized where it kept wandering.

Harriet Roberts, Psychotherapist

Tiffany said she'd found him crying in the gardener's shed. 'I told him, there's no need to get upset. It's only a *book*.' But he'd said something through his tears about his mother.

Then he'd clammed up.

We try not to let on when one of them is indiscreet about another. But in our next private session I did tackle Eddie. 'I know we've talked a lot about your mother, Lucy. But I want to go back to that a little.'

They're none of them stupid.

'I *told* Tiff not to tell you!' he said sullenly. 'She even promised.'

I shrugged, and batted on for quite a while, but we made almost no headway. So when the hour was up, I sent him off with homework.

'*Homework?*'

'Yes,' I said. 'You have to write a letter to your mum.'

'To Lucy?' The laugh was scornful. 'She's not right in the head. Can't even *listen* properly, let alone read.'

'She's never going to see it, Eddie.'

'Then what's the point?'

'It's therapeutic. You can be honest. You'll find that, once you start, it will be difficult to stop. It's harder than you think to write down lies.'

That caught his interest. 'Really? Why?'

'Not sure,' I said. 'But that is true. Try it. You'll see.'

Tiffany Dent

The three of us – Tod, me and Eddie – were in Eddie's room. Jean-Pierre had gone back home the week before, and no one else had been put in there yet. I was scrunched up against the skirting board, pretending to smoke, and we were breaking the rules by talking about Glasgow. Well, Tod was breaking the rules by telling us a story I had heard before about a mate of his scraping at sandstone walls with a nail file to get a powder he could fold in wraps and fob off as 'best golden brown' to make some money for his own next hit.

Eddie and I were breaking the rules by listening.

Then, in the waste bin, I saw this crumpled letter with the words *pathetic* and *faintest idea what love's supposed to mean.*

I just assumed that he'd been giving some secret girl-friend the flick, and I was interested. You see, I'd rather hoped he fancied me. (I certainly liked him.)

OK, so I admit, I sneaked the letter out of the bin into my pocket. It was a rotten thing to do, and I wished I hadn't later when I read it through. It was the nastiest letter I have ever read. So cold. So *angry*. He blamed this mum of his for *everything*. He called her weak and stupid. He said that he had spent years living in terror of bumping into Harris and that was her fault. *Everything* was her fault. He said he'd seen plenty of mothers managing on their own with babies and small children – even addict mothers. And all of them had done a better job than she had. He even said he thought that weakness like hers was a sin.

He said that. Honestly. He said it was a *sin*.

He said he didn't think that he could forgive her. Ever.

Harriet Roberts, Psychotherapist

I asked him how writing the letter went. (He hadn't brought it with him.)

He said he found it interesting. 'I spewed out quite a lot of stuff. Not what I thought I'd write at all.' He made a rueful face. 'It wasn't very nice.'

'No harm done,' I reminded him. 'Would you like to tell me about it?'

'No!' he said sharply. He studied his feet in sullen fashion for a while, then added, 'It was too awful. It was so awful that I threw it away.'

'Oh, well,' I said. 'How do you feel now?'

'Better,' he admitted. 'I thought about the things I wrote for quite a time. I think the letter was a little hard on her.' He studied his torn nails. 'I mean, if you judged me by what I did in Glasgow . . .'

He'd mentioned this so often. 'Stealing that blind woman's purse?'

'And kicking that kid for his chips.' His face contorted in the familiar way. 'Well, if you judged me just by that, you'd think that I was loathsome. Absolutely *loathsome*.'

'And you are not.'

'No. No, I'm not.' He leaned towards me. 'But, you see, Nicholas came to fetch me. In the middle of the night.' He waved a hand at the walls. 'And Natasha's paying for this. And this place costs a *fortune*.'

'It does indeed.'

'And Alice sends stuff every day – chocolates and post-cards and chewing gum. She even sends cartoons cut out of magazines.'

There was a long, long silence.

Then he whispered, 'I *try* to think that there was no one for my mum. No one at all. Then I could think she never had a chance.' The tears streamed down his face. 'But it's not *true*, is it? I mean, there's always *someone*. And she should have turned to them to keep me safe.'

I wasn't going to argue. I sat quietly.

He wiped both palms across his face. 'I'm fine with hating Harris. I know now that he was my proper father and I was only kidding myself with all that Mr Perkins stuff—'

'Not kidding yourself, Eddie. *Protecting* yourself. And very sensibly and very well.'

He brushed the interruption aside. 'Anyhow, I hate

him and I hope he's dead. I have no problem with that. I owe him nothing. Nothing at all!'

The tears kept coming. He kept wiping them away.

'But my mum's *different*. She didn't *start* like that. Like that first time that we watched Mr Perkins. I can remember she was *different*.'

He finished with a strangled sob.

We sat in silence for a little while. Then he spoke up again.

'You know that place I stayed in when I first went to Manchester—'

I glanced down at my notes. 'Barry and Jasmine?'

'Yes. *She* managed it all right. Jaz worried about *her* son, so she just kicked me out. No argument. Just *out*.'

Young people have to get through life. Sometimes you have to take a punt with a suggestion that might help.

'You've never wondered if your mum was horribly unlucky? That maybe she got punched too hard too soon to make a sensible decision?'

'You mean, she might have been already thinking we should leave? Planning it, even?'

'It's very possible.'

'And then, before she took the chance, he knocked her stupid?'

'The man did clearly pack a boxer's punch.'

He thought about it for a while. 'And after that – well, there was no one there to help – except for me.'

'You were too young to do a thing. A child that age simply assumes that's how life *is*.'

'You're saying maybe if she'd had someone who'd put out for her — like I had family?'

'Think of it this way, Eddie. Suppose you *hadn't* had family?'

I left him to think this one through. And then he said it. 'Maybe I would have ended up as drunk and vile as Harris.'

'That certainly seems to be where you were headed . . .'

His voice shook. 'Kicking kids . . . snatching blind people's stuff because they're easy meat.' Suddenly his eyes met mine. 'But that's not me!'

'I know it's not.'

'And I'm to try and think that wasn't her?'

'You said yourself, "She didn't start like that".'

'No,' he said. 'No, she didn't. Or she would never have remembered some of the words from the song.'

Seeing my puzzled look, he shook his head. 'It doesn't matter.'

There was no time in any case to set off down another path. So I just said, 'Well, Eddie, if you can feel a bit of sympathy for your mum, can't you forgive yourself?'

He told me bitterly, 'That's different. I had a working *brain*. And choices.'

'Not at the time,' I reminded him. 'That's what addiction *means*. But you will get on top of yourself again.'

'On top of myself!' He snorted. 'Sounds like a bloody mountain climb!'

I nearly said it. Yes, Eddie. Except it's harder, and takes far, far longer.

Eddie

I still had panic attacks. They'd push my head between my knees and I would use the trick that Linda taught me all those years ago – breathe out as slowly as I could, and count to ten. Her comforting soft strictures would echo through my mind. *'Steady, my poppet! Steady! You're safe now. He'll never get to you again. Now, come on, Eddie. Keep breathing. Slowly, slowly. There's my own precious baby. There's my boy . . .'*

One day when Dr Ross came round, I had a moan. 'I still can't concentrate. My brain's a *fug*.'

'How long have you been with us?' She glanced at my notes. 'Four weeks.' She tapped her pencil on her teeth and studied me a while. 'All right. I'm going to lower the dose. But if the staff report you're getting irritable or agitated, I shall increase it again.'

I tried to make a joke of it. 'Can I still bite my fingernails?'

She snorted. 'God! Are they no better?'

I stuck my hands out. She inspected what was left of my nails and shuddered. 'A *disgusting* habit. You might as well be shovelling germs into your mouth.'

Then we both laughed because we realized I was only there because I had been shovelling something fifty times worse into my mouth for months.

It was a while before I could read again. But when I could, I felt much better. I ploughed my way through *Sherlock Holmes*, and all the other books lying around the unit. Finally I started on the ones Natasha wanted me to read before I filled in the form. I was relieved to find I'd made as good a stab at choosing from the jacket covers as I would have from reading them all through.

It made me feel a little braver about what was coming.

And then, one day, I woke up happy.

I wasn't even thinking about anything.

I was just *happy*.

Tiffany

I told you that I really liked him. I liked him a *lot*.

I'd spent time in the unit twice before, so knew that when they think you're ready to go, they tell your parents but they don't tell you. You're chucked out really fast, before you've had the time to make arrangements to meet anyone. (It's in the rules that you give up your mobile even before you come, and never get that number back.)

So, when I overheard that cleaner saying, 'No need to

bother with that one today,' as he passed Eddie's room, I panicked.

Eddie was doing nothing in the telly room. I shut the door behind me. 'I reckon you're on standby. Want to give me your address?'

There was a little embarrassed pause. Then, 'No,' he said. 'Sorry, but I'm not going to tell you.'

I gave him a bit of a look.

'I'm sorry,' he said again. 'Honestly I am. But I want this to last.'

'But I'll be clear too, by the time that I get out.'

You could tell from his face that he'd been warned: *Watch out for Tiffany. This isn't her first visit.* (Translation: Probably won't be her last.)

We get a lecture on Free Will. I've heard it three times now. It basically says that there's a disagreement as to whether human beings make their own choices or not. But Harriet says that anyone who ends up here has more of a problem than other people about this. Habit has got us into one big mess, and we'll have to use habit to keep us out of it in future.

And that means stopping making certain choices. Instead, you simply follow rules that help you kick the habits you no longer want, and stick to ones you do.

I didn't argue with him. I just said, 'I'll be so *bored* without you. Can you at least leave me that weird old book of yours?'

Would you believe it? He said no to that.

Eddie

They try to bolster you up before you leave. 'Remember,' Dr Ross said. 'It's always HALT. It's HALT for life for you now, Eddie. All day and every day.'

HALT's one of their catchphrases. It stands for 'Never get too Hungry, Angry, Lonely or Tired.' That's when you crack and just don't care about breaking the rules.

It's hard to kick a habit. Keeping a habit off is even worse. The first night I was home, I thought about drink all the time. They tried to make it easy. When Alice dumped her book bag down on the side cabinet, the door swung open and I saw that they had cleared out every bottle. Only the mixers like the ginger ale were left. If Nicholas still had his gin and tonic every night, he didn't drink it anywhere near me. And every evening, one or another of them claimed to want me to go with them to see this film, or join them on a walk, or help them clear out the loft or the garage.

Everyone kept me busy. Natasha even hired a private tutor to bring me up to speed before the term began. I rather liked that. I found it soothing, sitting beside fat, comforting Mrs Maurdeff while she droned on about 'appropriate language for the task', and ticked me off for writing 'going off on one' when I meant 'losing my temper'. Stuff like that. I was reminded of all those years ago when I sat at the kitchen table with Linda folding her hand round mine to make me hold the pencil right, or pointing to the words in *Frog and Toad*.

But Alice helped the most. She didn't know it, and I wasn't going to tell her. But that idea she'd put into my head all those long months ago became a life-saver. Back then she'd yelled, 'You act as if you have some *beast* inside you!' And she had meant it. That's why I got so mad.

But it was true. I do have something of Bryce Harris deep inside, just as I have the look of him stamped on my face. He's my blood family, after all.

So I have learned a different way to use that. Whenever I need another, stronger reason for stopping wanting what I want, I think of him.

I think of him inside me. I even conjure up his voice. He used to roar and threaten way back then, when I was little. But now he's taken more to wheedling. 'Go on. You could have just one drink. No one will notice. It won't set you off. You've studied hard all day. You've *earned* it. Just one won't hurt. I don't believe you're telling me you're never going to have a drink again! Not even *one*? What sort of life is *that*?'

And I take my revenge. I answer back. I think of that bit of me that's come down from him and always will be him. The Beast. (I even call it that.) I like to think of it inside me, desperate to spend the day a different way — in pubs, one drink after another, then staggering home to sprawl among more beer cans.

I even stand in front of mirrors now and look him straight in the face. *My* face. I practically enjoy tormenting him.

'Just one,' I hear him tempt.

'No, thanks,' I say. 'Not having one to suit you.'

(Or, 'I don't drink.' Or, 'Get your own stuff. I'm not helping you.')

I like to feel him shrivelling up inside me, longing for alcohol, miserable, bored, *aching* for me to crack. The beast inside. He has a million reasons why I should buy one little bottle, just in case.

If he keeps on, I tell him, 'No. This is *you* wanting to have a drink, not *me*. And you're not having it.'

I've no idea if the real Harris is alive, or where he is. It matters less and less.

Not that the rest of it gets any easier. It's just I get more used to dealing with it. I can believe now that I can walk past a supermarket or a corner shop, and not go in. They told us in the clinic that different habits train your brain to go down different paths. They promised us that saying no over and over will gradually shift from being one huge effort that can leave you shaking to being easy.

Almost automatic.

'No thanks. I don't.'

I cannot wait for that day. Except, of course, I might miss bullying the beast because I feel I'm sticking up for Mum in standing up to him the way she never could. I'm guessing Harriet was right. Mum's luck was worse than mine. I've got a life ahead. She took one knock too many, and there's nothing left. I go to visit her, and I amuse myself by telling her about my friends. Poor Lucy can't keep any of their names straight in her head. She doesn't even try. She smiles and nods. I smile and nod back, and we talk of cake and colours. And that works.

Natasha asked me if I wanted to invite my mother to the big dinner she arranged at Valentine House the night we celebrated my exam results. (I'd done so well, they made a thing of it.) But I said no. Everyone else came. Linda and Alan. Alice. They even raked up Rob. All people who had helped along the way.

Linda got squiffy and a little tearful towards the end. She said it was a shame that Mr Perkins couldn't be there too – that he had done the most. She wanted me to sing one of his songs with her. 'People sing "Happy Birthday" in restaurants,' she kept on saying. 'Why shouldn't we sing "Happy Days"?'

She tried quite hard to wheedle me into it. But I was firm. I didn't want to go along with the idea. (For all I knew, someone else celebrating in that restaurant might have been going off to study the same course as me.) But I did squeeze her hand the way she used to squeeze mine. And we did hum it quietly together.

I looked across the table and saw Natasha smiling.

She raised her glass to me.

And I raised my glass back.

Also by Anne Fine:

THE DEVIL WALKS

Since the day he was born, Daniel has been hidden
away from the outside world. Told that he suffers from
a mysterious illness, only a knock at the door reveals
just how many secrets his reclusive mother has kept
from him. Yet Daniel cannot understand what she
has tried to protect him from so desperately.

Torn from his home, he begins to piece together the
chilling truth – a dark legacy of vicious cruelty and
fiendish spite that has held his family in its grip for years.

'A superb and subtle writer' *Guardian*

'A pitch-perfect Gothic thriller' *Sunday Telegraph*

Also by Anne Fine:

THE BOOK OF THE BANSHEE

It's war . . .

Will has two sisters. Muffy - a little angel who loves
bedtime stories. And Estelle. A screaming, screeching
banshee whose moods explode through the household.

Mum and Dad are battling on.
And Will feels as if he's living on the front line . . .

'It is humorous. It is witty.
It is brilliant!' *Daily Mail*

Also by Anne Fine:

THE GRANNY PROJECT

Negotiation – or blackmail?

Mum and Dad reckon things would be
better if Granny were in a Home.

The kids all want her to stay.

Ivan's Granny Project should make his parents think
again. But there's more than one way of doing a project.
And blackmail can work two ways . . .

SHORTLISTED FOR THE GUARDIAN
CHILDREN'S FICTION AWARD

'Crisp, funny and refreshingly satirical' *Guardian*